I0552234

First published in 2025.

ISBN (ebook): 978-1-7644573-4-7
ISBN (paperback): 978-1-7644573-5-4
ISBN (hardcover): 978-1-7644573-6-1

Cost of Consent

A Psychological Thriller

J. X. Miller

Table of Contents

Chapter One

---∞---

The Removal

T he operating room was quiet before Jax entered it, not silent, quiet, as machines waited in low suspension and monitors idled at baseline, instruments arranged with deliberate spacing, each aligned toward the center of the field, nothing improvised, nothing decorative, the room prepared by people who knew her preferences and followed them exactly.

Jax paused at the threshold, as she always did, not out of ritual but verification, because the room told her what kind of day this would be, today clean, today ready.

Before she scrubbed, she read the chart again, not the summary but the notes beneath it, the intake forms, the prior discharges, the places where language softened into administration and harm became a category instead of a fact.

A consent page sat clipped to the surgical pack, printed and countersigned, and beneath it was a second document on newer hospital letterhead with a blank field marked for third-party reporting, which Jax tapped once with a gloved finger.

"What is this?" she asked, and the circulating nurse glanced down and said that finance had added it, that it was now standard for external funding, to which Jax replied that it was not standard for her cases, prompting the nurse to offer to remove it and Jax to tell her to do so, after which the document was slid aside with no argument and no delay.

Jax washed in without conversation while the team assembled around her with the economy of habit, no one speaking unless spoken to because noise created error, error created hesitation, and hesitation was the one thing she would not tolerate.

The patient was already positioned, head fixed and body draped, only the skull visible, marked and measured, planning lines traced across bone with mathematical neatness as Jax reviewed them again anyway, and she did not rush.

The patient was a woman in her early thirties with a history of prolonged psychological trauma extending back more than a decade, with multiple episodes across multiple environments and symptoms resistant to conventional treatment across three institutions, medication, therapy, and exposure protocols having failed, leaving a record that was extensive and unambiguous.

There were no contraindications for surgery and no neurological abnormalities outside the targeted region, consent having been obtained, reviewed, and re-obtained, because consent mattered to Jax even when it slowed scheduling, even when administrators complained about throughput, and even when colleagues argued that her results justified efficiency, especially then.

She stepped closer to the patient, lowering her voice though the woman was already under light sedation, and began to confirm understanding of what was about to happen, that memory would not be removed but only intensity, that more relief was possible than she would provide and that she would stop short of that point, that she was choosing restraint rather than limitation, and that the patient could refuse at any time before full anesthesia for any reason, waiting until a nod became speech and the patient said she understood.

Jax held her gaze, not looking for fear but for comprehension and the capacity to withdraw, and told her that if she wanted her to stop she must say so even if it felt too late, correcting the patient's instinctive refusal with the reminder that it was only a prediction, until the patient said, more slowly, that if she wanted her to stop she would tell her, which Jax accepted as sufficient before straightening and turning to the team and telling them to begin.

Anesthesia deepened gradually as monitors brightened and numbers appeared, respiration stabilizing as sedation progressed without resistance, while the anesthetist adjusted the drip and said she was steady, Jax replying that she needed to remain steady with no spikes, that flat was not the goal and responsive was, and when he asked if she was still concerned about blunting she answered that she was concerned about absence, returning his attention to the monitor without further discussion.

Jax reviewed the imaging again, as she always did, noting that the target region was small, that this was the point, because she did not remove trauma but amplification and the distinction mattered, even as a junior registrar watched too closely and remarked that she could take more, to which she replied that she could but would not, not because of risk but because of consequence, not to outcome but to agency, a distinction he did not yet understand.

She had seen what happened when surgeons treated relief as a target rather than a boundary, one colleague calling it compassion and the patient calling it peace, only for six months later to bring a person who no longer refused, no longer left rooms, no longer ended conversations, no longer recognized pressure as pressure, a file Jax herself had closed after refusing follow-up surgery and being called conservative for it.

She took the scalpel and made the incision cleanly, blood controlled immediately and the field opening as expected nothing surprising and therefore good, as she worked methodically layer by layer with economical movement, no wasted motion, and no adjustment for comfort because comfort came later.

As she exposed the skull her attention narrowed and the world reduced to structure, depth, and alignment, a place where rules were fixed and cause and effect behaved, the drill engaging as sound changed and pressure was applied, bone yielding predictably and the opening measured again before proceeding.

Inside the skull the brain rested as it always did, unremarkable and vulnerable and capable of extraordinary cruelty to itself, as she adjusted the microscope and leaned in on the dense cluster of tissue mapped over years, over failures, over patients she had refused to operate on when the risk of flattening response outweighed relief, patients she did not think about now as she began the excision.

Her hands were steady as tissue was removed incrementally and response markers were checked continuously, the monitors adjusting and subtle changes registering as the brain responded as expected, until at a certain point she slowed and at another point she stopped, knowing without measuring that this was the line beyond which relief would deepen but resistance would flatten, fear receding along with refusal.

She withdrew the instrument and observed as the numbers stabilized, waiting while the anesthetist glanced at her and then back to the monitors, no one speaking until Jax nodded once and told them to close, the team sealing the opening and restoring layers as the incision closed with minimal trauma and the patient was prepared for recovery.

Jax stepped back and removed her gloves, not watching the final suturing because that part was complete, leaving the room without ceremony and entering a recovery ward that smelled of antiseptic and warmth with machines humming at a lower register, where she stood at the foot of the bed and waited.

The patient's eyes opened slowly as disorientation passed quickly, the mind recalibrating faster when it was no longer under siege, and when Jax asked if she could hear her the answer came steady with no tremor or urgency, no pain and no distress after a brief analytical pause, as Jax waited longer than most clinicians would have, watching micro expressions, delays, and absences before asking how she felt.

The patient described a quiet, as though something had stepped back, which Jax said was expected, explaining that nothing was gone but contained, and as the patient accepted this without visible reaction Jax continued the assessment, not the checklist but the markers that mattered, asking what she had agreed to before coming into the room and hearing that it was the surgery and that she would stop early, that if she did not she would be wrong, and that if that happened the patient would tell someone even though she could not yet say who.

Jax noted that absence of routing, not fear and not confusion, and tested further by asking what she would do if someone made her uncomfortable, hearing that she would ask them to stop, that she would leave if they did not, and that she would tell someone if she could not, responses delivered with no urgency and no distress, even as two more variations confirmed the same pattern, correct but delayed.

Satisfied, Jax stepped back and told her she would be monitored closely, daily at first, acknowledging the faint smile and the expression of trust with a nod rather than a reply before turning and leaving.

Her office was small and functional with no personal effects beyond what was unavoidable, files stacked neatly and screens clean, the space reflecting her priorities as she dictated notes in clinical, controlled language that recorded the outcome as consistent with expectations, no adverse events, early indicators positive, boundary recognition present with delay, escalation routing absent, adding instructions to monitor longitudinal agency markers and compare them to baseline pre-operative refusal latency before stopping the recording.

Her screen refreshed to reveal a dashboard of aggregate outcomes, comparative metrics, and financial overlays, which made her frown because she had not authorized external reporting, followed by a second dashboard of trend projections, cost curves, and a column labelled utilisation that briefly opened to a restricted list before closing again.

Her phone buzzed and she ignored it, then another buzz came with an email notification whose subject line was neutral and institutional, requesting an outcomes discussion from a sender not clinical but finance adjacent, followed by another from hospital administration announcing new reporting requirements for external partners, messages she did not open because the subject lines were enough, before a further notification arrived marked funding inquiry and confidential.

Jax stared at the screen longer this time, having expected interest but not immediacy, knowing that anything which reduced suffering without visible cost attracted attention, especially from those tasked with measuring cost, and as she walked to the window she watched the city below moving in patterns of systems functioning and people operating until they failed, the problem with success being that it made things legible.

Her phone rang and she answered it, hearing a calm, professional voice introduce itself as Marcus Hale representing a consortium interested in her work, explaining that they had been reviewing her outcomes and found them impressive and, more importantly, consistent, because consistency mattered more than efficacy.

He said they would like to discuss supporting her program by expanding access and protecting it, to which Jax replied that protection implied threat, while Marcus clarified that it meant instability rather than malice, and when Jax said that support came with expectations he agreed that it always did, outlining financial, administrative, and legal support while confirming that clinical control would remain hers, an answer that was correct, perhaps too correct.

When Jax asked about expectations he listed outcomes, transparency, and standardization, a word that settled heavily as she said she did not optimise but intervened, Marcus replying that he knew and that it was why they were calling, before proposing a meeting at her convenience, accepting her request to send details and closing with the assurance that it was not about control but sustainability, a word that carried weight as Jax ended the call.

That evening she reviewed patient data again, not only the day's case but all of them, seeing patterns that were clean, too clean, with relief curves flattening rapidly and reactivity dampening predictably as function returned across cohorts, everything she had aimed for, and she reviewed earlier cases of patients she had refused to operate on and those who had requested deeper excision, their files marked unresolved and chronic before she closed them.

One thought surfaced uninvited, that function was not the same as choice, which she dismissed as premature because pattern without data was sentiment, yet she wrote it down anyway and slid the note into a drawer for later.

The patient slept through the night without nightmares and in the days that followed reported no flashbacks, no panic, and no intrusion, returning to work within a week as her file was marked improved, while Jax watched the update appear on her screen without feeling satisfaction, only accuracy, and that would have to be enough.

Chapter Two

⬦⬦⬦

Proof of Success

T he first dataset arrived forty-eight hours after the procedure, not because Jax had asked for it but because it appeared where it should not have been, folded into her dashboard under a neutral heading that had not existed the week before, Aggregate Outcomes, which she opened once, scanned for structure, and then closed again because she preferred to work from individual cases outward, knowing that patterns mattered only after anomalies were understood and that averages hid mistakes.

Still, the data did not go away, and by the end of the week it had multiplied as a second tab appeared, then a third, then a fourth, each stamped with an internal code she did not recognize, with tables, comparisons, and baselines, a column labelled pre-intervention burden, another labelled functional recovery window, and a third, new and unqualified, labelled sustained capacity, a word that made her frown.

Capacity was not a term she used because it implied optimisation, and she intervened to reduce harm rather than enhance output, the word belonging to consultants and underwriters rather than surgeons, even as she opened the file anyway and saw early results that were clean, with sleep restoration across the cohort, reduced startle response, lower reported distress, return-to-work timelines compressed ahead of forecast, disability claims marked resolved, and medication tapering accelerated, all of it inside expected variance and defensible.

What unsettled her was not the numbers but the narrative welded to them, effective, durable, predictable, a word that was new, and when she clicked into the attached notes she found they were administrative rather than clinical, written by someone trained to summarize without nuance, describing the intervention as a stabilizing mechanism to reduce volatility and return individuals to baseline participation, without saying participation in what.

Jax closed the notes and opened the raw line items, scrolling until she found last week's patient by matching the masked identifiers to the date and theatre code, seeing outcome fields already populated with Improved, Stable, and Resolved, a word that was wrong because trauma did not resolve but reconfigured, quieted, retreated, and waited, while resolved implied an end point that systems used to justify neglect.

She highlighted the word and replaced it with contained in her own note field, saving the change even though it did not alter the dashboard and only altered her record, and when the word returned the next morning she opened the audit history only to find her access restricted, able to see that a change had been made but not by whom, prompting her to shut the laptop and walk to theatre where work still behaved, offering the comfort of instruments, sterility, anatomy, and a line you could draw and stop at.

After surgery she returned to her office to find a calendar invite waiting, short notice with senior attendees and no agenda, which she accepted, heading to a meeting room on a higher floor with glass walls, a long table, water already poured, and three people waiting, two she recognized from hospital operations and risk and compliance, the third introducing himself as finance with a title that suggested strategy.

They thanked her first, praising outcomes, discipline, and consent, one of them saying restraint twice as if to signal respect, before turning to demand as referrals increased internally and externally, external providers made enquiries, patients requested transfers, and a small number of interstate clinicians asked for guidance on eligibility criteria.

"We need to keep this safe," the risk representative said, to which Jax replied that it was safe because it was controlled, prompting agreement from him and a nod from finance that what they wanted was control and sustainability, a word that appeared again as Jax waited.

The operations lead slid a draft protocol across the table, her language copied into it in places and replaced by softer terms in others, less refusal and more alignment, and when she reached the section on reporting she noted external reporting, hearing assurances that it would be only aggregated and only with consent, though too quickly, leading her to tap the page and say that assumption was not consent.

Risk leaned forward and said they were not trying to corner her but protect her from misuse, from replication outside her thresholds, from people who would remove more because it looked better in a chart, while Jax looked at finance and named funding, which he did not deny, describing partners willing to underwrite expansion, cover theatre time, staff, monitoring, and follow-up, the things that kept her work honest.

Partners, she said, corrected by finance to stakeholders, and she did not ask for names because systems did not need them to apply force, instead asking what they got, to which risk replied reduced relapse, reduced crisis presentations, and reduced long-term burden, operations added more access, and finance added predictability, a word that made Jax keep her face neutral because predictability was a financial virtue rather than a clinical one.

She pointed to language calling the work capacity-restoring, and when operations called it a way to communicate value Jax said it misrepresented the aim, finance countering that words mattered, that her terms would confuse external bodies while theirs would fund it, to which Jax replied that funding brought attempts to own it, even if finance framed that as measurement with better manners.

Jax closed the document and set conditions, that clinical control remained hers, reporting required explicit consent, and outcome language stayed clinical without performance framing, hearing agreement from risk and operations and a slight hesitation from finance before he said they could align, a word that meant surrender.

The meeting ended without signatures but her program had shifted from experiment to asset in a single hour, and when she returned to her office the dashboard had updated again, capacity moved to a subheading, recovery paired with participation, distress reduction paired with stability, and in the underlying reports a new template attached to each case file with fields for Work Status, Coverage Status, and Return-to-Duty Clearance, fields that did not belong in her practice.

She filtered the cohort by those new fields, finding most blank but some already populated, completed, approved, and cleared, without recognizable author tags or access to the audit trail, so she printed the list and walked to the ward where Elena was scheduled for follow-up, arriving early to have the conversation before anyone coached it.

Elena sat upright with hands folded, calm posture, clean clothes, hair pinned back, prepared to be evaluated, and when Jax asked how she had been she said really good, describing sleeping through the night, leaving the house without scanning exits, returning calls without rehearsing, and going to the supermarket without a plan, adding that her hours had been increased and she had accepted a project.

When Jax asked whether she wanted it Elena paused briefly and analytically before saying it made sense because she was capable now, capable of handling things without getting stuck, and when Jax asked what she did when something felt uncomfortable Elena smiled slightly and said it did not feel that way anymore, prompting Jax to note that it was not an answer.

Elena said she dealt with it and it passed, her eyes showing no tremor, evasion, or defensive posture, a correct tone and a correct answer, until Jax asked what she had refused this week and Elena blinked at the word before saying nothing, that there had been nothing to refuse, which Jax wrote down.

When asked if anyone had asked her to do something she did not want, Elena mentioned the project, saying she would have said no if she had not wanted it, and when Jax asked why she said yes Elena replied that it was better and that she could, though better was an outcome rather than a reason.

Jax ended the interview with standard checks on sleep, appetite, medication, and intrusive thought frequency, all improved and all clean, which was the problem, and in the corridor a nurse approached with a clipboard bearing a return-to-work clearance form with Elena's name and a line for clinician approval, which Jax refused to sign because it was not her form, hearing that it was required now by admin and insurance, which the nurse called partnership in a lowered voice.

Jax told her she would not sign that day, leaving the nurse to seek clarification, and back in her office another email waited with the subject Success Metrics Alignment from a generic distribution list, which she did not open, instead opening raw patient files to read free-text notes where in three files she found the same phrase, patient reports increased willingness to comply with demands.

She searched the cohort for comply and found nine instances, then twelve, then fourteen, some phrased positively as compliance with treatment, workplace expectations, and legal processes, the tone celebratory as the word sat inside success, prompting her to write private notes stating that compliance was not the goal but an output and to verify agency, notes invisible to the dashboard but important to her.

That afternoon Marcus Hale emailed again, short and polite, thanking her for making time, saying he understood her caution, and that her work would be misused without her involvement, that he preferred honesty about incentives, asking to meet at a neutral location with no agenda for thirty minutes, which she ignored for two hours before accepting.

They met in the same quiet café without hovering staff or documents, Marcus beginning by asking why her stopping point was where it was, and when Jax said that beyond it patients lost something they could not name he nodded and said refusal, explaining that most systems treated refusal as friction to be removed while he knew she did not, that this was why he asked.

He spoke of harm minimization and systems that failed not from evil but from optimising the wrong variables, saying her work corrected a structural blind spot by reducing volatility for people who thought in risk curves, though Jax said she was not interested in their curves, even if they were interested in her.

He framed expansion as containment, warning that without her involvement others would replicate her work badly and without formal structures thresholds would erode, saying she was not responsible for the system but that she was its only brake, prompting Jax to ask about his role, which he described as being between, translating incentive into language she could use so she could set conditions that survived the meeting.

Conditions and survive were chosen carefully, and though she did not like him she recognized competence and restraint, asking directly who had asked him to call, hearing that it was a consortium rather than one company, and when she asked what they wanted he said predictability, flattened claims curves, high-functioning people back at work, faster courts, and fewer long-term liabilities.

When Jax asked what he wanted Marcus paused personally rather than strategically and said he wanted it done with her thresholds because without her it would be done without them, and as Jax looked out the window at people walking with phones in hand, function everywhere and consent invisible, she said that if she agreed to expansion it would not be because she trusted them but because she would not let them do it badly, a reason Marcus called the right one.

She told him to send the conditions he believed would hold, and he nodded without celebration, as if the choice had always been inevitable, and that evening back in her office Jax reviewed the dashboards again, seeing language shift so that recovery paired with restoration, distress reduction with stability, and stability with capacity.

She added a private addendum stating that expansion was accepted conditionally with clinical discretion retained, explicit consent, no performance framing, and no coercive prerequisites, saving it even though the dashboard did not change, and that night she reviewed the cohort again, every patient showing improvement with no red flags, adverse events, or complaints as the system responded exactly as designed.

Jax closed the files and sat back, telling herself that protection required scale, that without structure harm would multiply elsewhere, and that if this was going to happen it was better she remained inside it, typing the word Scalable before pausing and replacing it with Sustainable, leaving it there.

Chapter Three

———— ∞ ————

The Shield

M arcus Hale arrived ten minutes early and chose a table that gave him a clear view of the door without placing his back to the window, a posture that did not read as defensive but as practiced, which Jax noticed immediately as he stood to greet her, offered a polite nod, and waited for her to sit before taking his own seat, no handshake and no forced familiarity, letting her set the temperature.

"You picked this place," Jax said, and when Marcus replied that it was neutral with no affiliations she noted that it had been intentional, to which he simply agreed, the two of them ordering coffee and waiting until it arrived before he spoke again.

Marcus said he had read her published work, not the summaries but the appendices, and that she was unusually explicit about what she refused to do, that most clinicians wrote toward outcomes while she wrote toward limits, which she answered by saying limits kept people human, Marcus nodding that they also made systems nervous even if she said that was not her problem, a point he accepted while adding that it became her problem when systems decided to route around her.

Jax studied him, noticing that he was careful with words without being evasive, that he did not posture or flatter, and when she asked why he was there he considered the question before answering that her work was already being classified, that she had not started the process but was now inside it.

When she asked how it was being classified he replied that it was stabilizing, capacity restoring, low variance, terms that tightened her mouth because they were not clinical but actuarial, and when she said his admiration did not sound like admiration he explained that it was precisely because she was not doing what they wanted but what they could use, a description rather than an accusation.

Jax asked who they were, and Marcus described a consortium rather than a single insurer, health, disability, workers compensation, and legal exposure carriers intersecting around long tail risk, saying that he advised them by translating between clinical reality and institutional appetite, a role that sounded like control to Jax and like leverage to him, because control came later if no one intervened.

When Jax noted that he was intervening he agreed, saying he believed her thresholds mattered, explaining that when systems adopted innovation they removed friction, flattened variance, and rewarded predictability until anything that introduced refusal was smoothed out, which was why refusal was the point, and why he was telling her that she was the only person positioned to slow it down without being sidelined, even if that felt like pressure not coming from him.

She asked why him, and Marcus spoke of his early career inside one of the firms doing risk modelling and behavioral forecasting, watching a pattern repeat as people were cleared faster, returned to work sooner, claims closed cleanly, and courts moved, everyone congratulating themselves until five years later those same people reappeared in different datasets, not broken or distressed but absorbent, taking on more responsibility, exposure, and risk without complaint or resistance, praised until they collapsed quietly with no incident, no breach, and no villain.

Jax called it a story rather than proof, and Marcus called it a pattern, saying proof came later after people had been used, which led her to look down at her cup without drinking and note that he had left, something he confirmed because once a pattern became profitable it stopped being treated as a problem.

When she said that now he helped them he answered that he helped them understand when to stop, not because he was optimistic but pragmatic, knowing that systems stopped only when the cost of continuation exceeded the cost of restraint, which was why he thought she was not the restraint but the justification, because without her restraint looked arbitrary and with her it looked principled.

Jax's fingers tightened around the cup as she said he wanted her to legitimize them, and Marcus countered that he wanted her to constrain them, warning that if she refused to engage they would engage someone else who would call optimisation compassion, and that her work was not the first intervention that made people easier to manage but the first that looked ethical enough to scale, which was why the framing mattered.

When she asked what he actually did he described sitting in rooms where risk was translated into money, telling people what their models could not capture, where their incentives created hidden liability, and pushing for guardrails because guardrails were cheaper than scandal, documenting when they ignored him and deciding whether to stay, go, or route, choosing where harm would occur when a decision was inevitable.

Jax said he was describing compromise as morality, and Marcus said he was describing compromise as the only tool a system recognized, that her morality was what he was trying to preserve, and when she asked why she should trust him he answered that she should not yet, that he was offering information rather than trust.

She asked who had initiated contact, and Marcus said hospital administration had requested a risk assessment, the consortium an external view, and that he had been selected because he did not sell surgery as a product, adding that what they wanted was predictability, flattened variance, shorter claims tails, faster clearance, and fewer long-term liabilities, which was insurance rather than medicine.

When Jax asked what he wanted Marcus paused personally and said he wanted her thresholds to survive contact with the system, because without them it would become something else, and that he also wanted her protected because he knew what happened to the person who became the face of a machine, first praised and then blamed, a symbol if it worked and a sacrifice if it failed.

He said a shield was only useful if placed early, and Jax sat in silence recognizing that he was selling risk management rather than hope, asking him to clarify thresholds, which he defined as her stopping point, her refusal to sign coercive prerequisites, and her insistence on explicit consent, things systems did not respect unless they were expensive to cross, something he could try to make happen through governance language, contracts, and protocols that triggered audits.

Jax repeated the word audits, hearing that systems did not fear ethics but review, leading her to call the answer bureaucracy and him to call it friction, the way choice was preserved inside machines, as Jax looked past him at people moving outside with heads down and phones in hand, function everywhere and consent invisible.

She stated that she would not optimise and that she would not create language equating recovery with productivity, nor allow treatment to become a prerequisite for coverage, to which Marcus replied that the last was the hardest and therefore the most likely to be attempted, though not always successfully.

When Jax said he was telling her to join them so she could resist them he answered that she was already in their line of sight, easier to sideline from the outside and harder to remove from within, though stepping in would make her complicit, a cost he acknowledged, saying he was not comfortable but trained by outcomes and by watching people harmed by clean reports.

Jax asked why not expose it, and Marcus said exposure required an audience willing to listen, which the beneficiaries of this system were not, and when she raised patients he said they wanted relief, and relief was real, which was what made it dangerous, because false harm would be easy to fight.

They finished their coffee without ceremony, and when they stood Marcus did not ask for another meeting or push for commitment, only saying he would send conditions rather than contracts, guardrails and trigger points, language that would hold up in rooms full of people who did not care about intent, which Jax said she might ignore, a response he accepted as reasonable.

As she walked back toward the hospital Jax replayed not his words but his assumptions, that the system could be bent, slowed, and made to pay for crossing a line, unsure if he was right but knowing he had not lied or promised what he could not guarantee.

That night she opened a new document and drafted her own conditions, not for the consortium but for herself, no optimisation, no coercion, no prerequisite framing, explicit consent at every stage, audit visibility, and clinical veto, stopping at the last line, no silent transfer of responsibility, leaving the document open and unsaved.

The next morning Marcus's email arrived without attachments, only a short note stating that he was not there to decide for her but to make sure she was not decided for, which Jax read twice before closing the laptop.

———— ∞ ————

Chapter Four

After Care

E lena woke before the alarm and lay still, waiting for the familiar surge that used to follow consciousness, the tightening in her chest, the inventory of exits, the quick arithmetic of risk, but nothing came. Her body felt neutral, not calm and not safe, neutral, as if a signal had been muted rather than solved.

She stared at the ceiling and tested the silence deliberately, replaying the images that once triggered panic. The memories remained intact and the response did not arrive, not courage, not healing, absence. When she sat up her heart rate stayed even, no shallow breath, no heat in the face, no tremor in the hands, and the lack of reaction registered as relief without pleasure, procedural, like a system returning to baseline after prolonged overload.

In the kitchen she made coffee without rushing and drank it standing at the counter while strolling through her phone, three messages from work, one calendar reminder, one message from her sister asking if she was still coming on Sunday. Elena answered all of them immediately, quick confirmations that surprised her because before every reply required rehearsal and a wrong word could invite a wrong outcome, but now words arrived as if the path had been cleared.

She dressed quickly, not carefully, no longer choosing clothes based on who might look at her, choosing what was clean as function replaced calculation. Outside, the street looked unchanged, cars moved and people walked, and Elena stepped into it without scanning faces. She still noticed everyone, but it did not matter in the way it used to.

At work she arrived early and took the desk nearest the window, not positioning herself with her back to the wall, not checking where the security cameras were, not watching the corridor in peripheral vision while pretending to focus on her screen. She opened her laptop and made a simple list without contingencies or escape plans, just work.

Her manager stopped by mid-morning and noted she was early, Elena replying that she woke up. He smiled, uncertain whether she was joking, but she was not, and when he saw her screen, he said she was already into it before lowering his voice as if the request was a favor. There was a new project, he said, something that needed someone steady, someone who didn't get knocked around by noise, cross functional, high visibility, fast turnaround, and then he asked if she wanted it.

Elena waited only long enough to register the question. "I can take it," she said, and the decision came cleanly, not brave, and not coerced, correct. Her manager's shoulders loosened and he told her he knew she was the right pick, a phrase Elena stored without reacting.

By lunch she had created a task list and assigned owners, by afternoon she had scheduled a kickoff call, speaking in that call without hesitation, not apologizing for taking space and not asking permission to lead. People responded to her tone, calm, direct, certain.

That night her manager forwarded an email praising her efficiency and cc'd a senior executive, using the word resilient twice. Elena read it and felt nothing, which surprised her because before the procedure, praise produced anxiety, attention triggered vigilance, compliments felt like hooks, and now they passed through as information, received and filed with no residue.

On the way home she called her sister. "You sound different," her sister said, and Elena answered that she was better. When her sister asked in what way, Elena paused because the question felt imprecise, requiring an emotional vocabulary she no longer needed, and she said she didn't get stuck anymore. Her sister asked if she was happy, Elena considered before admitting she didn't know, she didn't feel bad, and her sister laughed softly, calling it an upgrade. They spoke about the family gathering Elena had avoided for two years, and Elena accepted without resistance, saying she would be there as a fact rather than a promise.

On Saturday morning Elena went to the supermarket without planning a route or checking exits, not carrying a list in her head as if it were a shield. When a man stepped too close in the aisle she adjusted her position without flinching, no surge of fear and no irritation, and continued selecting produce. She completed her shopping and left, and the absence of reaction felt like strength.

At her follow-up appointment she sat upright across from Dr. Nile, hands folded and posture aligned, looking like someone prepared to be evaluated. Jax asked how she had been, and Elena said good, really good, describing sleep through the night, leaving the house without scanning exits, returning calls without rehearsing responses, taking on a new project, speaking in meetings, and Jax listened without interruption.

"And when something feels uncomfortable," Jax asked, "what do you do."

Elena smiled faintly. "It doesn't really feel that way anymore."

"That was not the question," Jax said, and Elena considered before answering that she dealt with it and it passed.

Jax watched her closely and asked what Elena had refused that week, the word refusing itself sounding strange in Elena's mouth when she repeated it back. Jax pressed her to name anything, something, and Elena searched for her memory until she admitted nothing, there was nothing to refuse, and Jax wrote something down.

Jax asked whether anyone had asked Elena to do something she did not want to do, and Elena hesitated before mentioning the project. Jax asked what Elena would have done if she did not want it, and Elena answered that she would have said no, then Jax asked why she said yes and Elena said she could handle it, it made sense. The answers were coherent and empty, and when Jax asked about boundaries, discomfort, disagreement, whether Elena had raised her voice, ended a conversation, walked away, Elena responded evenly, no distress, no emotional charge.

When the appointment ended Elena left with a follow-up schedule and a mild sense of efficiency, not gratitude and not dependency, trusting the outcome because trust felt neutral now.

Back at work the pace increased and the new project expanded, a deadline moved forward, two stakeholders demanded progress updates, and Elena absorbed the pressure without resistance. She stopped checking the time, stayed late without noticing fatigue, and when a colleague missed a deliverable Elena compensated without complaint, without asking why, without setting a boundary, solving the problem. Her manager praised her again, calling her unshakeable, and Elena nodded and said she was fine, hearing unshakeable as both compliment and designation.

A week later HR requested a conversation framed as positive; talent development, leadership potential, opportunity, and Elena attended without anxiety. The HR representative smiled too broadly and spoke about growth, resilience, and how Elena's recent trajectory had been noticed, saying they liked what they were seeing and that Elena had responded incredibly well. When Elena asked her to elaborate the representative pointed to performance, engagement, steadiness, then introduced a development track requiring flexibility, travel sometimes, longer hours, but a pathway, and Elena agreed without asking about workload or personal limits.

"You're very decisive," the representative said.

"It makes sense," Elena replied.

"That's what we love," the representative said, laughing lightly.

When Elena walked back to her desk, she noticed an email marked confidential from the insurance liaison attached to the company, subject line Coverage Review and Recovery Confirmation. She opened it and found congratulatory, efficient language, thanking her for participating in treatment, noting that her recovery had been recorded as successful and that her file required routine updating, with a link to forms. Elena clicked and began completing them, confirming she felt capable of returning to pre incident function, selecting no for accommodations, consenting to future assessments if required, and selecting no for relapse indicators including avoidance, irritability, or refusal to attend work. The word refusal appeared again as a symptom, and Elena did not pause, submitting the forms and returning to her tasks.

At the family gathering on Sunday Elena arrived on time and her sister hugged her tightly, relieved that she was there. People spoke loudly, children ran, someone dropped a plate, and Elena did not startle or retreat to a corner. An uncle approached and asked about the incident in a casual tone, as if it were a story he owned, and Elena listened. Before the procedure, his tone would have triggered heat in her face and made her leave the room, but now it registered as rude without landing as threat. She answered plainly, saying it happened, and she was fine, and her uncle smiled, relieved by the simplicity, telling her he was glad she was over it. Elena agreed, noting that over it was wrong, but wrongness no longer carried weight, just incorrect data.

Later her cousin asked if Elena could help plan an event and Elena agreed immediately, more tasks and more responsibility accepted as if there were no cost. When Elena and her sister were alone her sister asked if she was sure, reminding her that she used to agree and panic later, and Elena paused, the memory existing as fact without sensation, saying she wouldn't panic. Her sister studied her face and said she looked calm, and Elena replied that she was.

The following week the project entered crisis, a vendor pulled out, the deadline remained, stakeholders demanded solutions, and Elena organized a recovery plan in a single afternoon. Her manager told her she was saving the program with gratitude that carried dependence and asked her to hold it for a few more weeks. Elena agreed, noticing the phrase need you but receiving it as a request rather than a trap. She took on more, stopped leaving on time, ate lunch at her desk, drank coffee late into the evening, and when her body signaled fatigue, the signal was faint and easy to ignore.

A colleague pulled her aside and said she didn't have to do all of it, that they were using her, that she used to push back and say no, and Elena searched herself before answering that no wasn't necessary if the outcome was correct. The colleague stared at her and said that wasn't how people lived, and Elena returned to her desk and kept working.

That evening an email arrived again from the insurance liaison with a new form and a brief note that ongoing coverage depended on documented participation in recovery maintenance. Elena read the sentence twice, the phrase depended on triggering - not fear but action, and she completed the form immediately.

The next day a meeting was scheduled with a senior executive, framed as career progression, and Elena arrived on time. The executive congratulated her, spoke about resilience, and said the organisation valued people who could absorb pressure without destabilizing, asking whether she would travel for a week to fix an issue in another office. Elena agreed, and the executive smiled and said people like her didn't say no, a sentence delivered lightly like praise. Elena nodded and did not challenge it, leaving the room with a small delay in her steps, as if her mind registered something that did not convert into emotion. People like you.

Two weeks later a compliance officer requested a meeting using neutral language, routine, alignment, documentation update, and Elena attended in a small room with a single camera in the corner. The officer smiled too politely and placed a folder on the table, saying they were updating Elena's risk profile and that it was a positive update. She said there was evidence of sustained recovery, that treatment had been recorded as successful, and that it changed how certain protections applied, then corrected herself to special arrangements, flexible scheduling, restricted travel, additional approvals.

"If you're fully restored," the officer said, "those adjustments are no longer necessary, it's good news."

Elena nodded again, understanding that good news was the category assigned to removal. The officer slid a form toward her and said it confirmed Elena no longer required accommodations and helped keep the file clean, and Elena read it once. The language was simple, stable, capable, fit, and she signed. The compliance officer thanked her and said it reduced friction for everyone, and Elena stored the word without reacting.

After that, her manager stopped asking whether she could take on extra work and began assigning it as default. A new project arrived without discussion, another deadline, another cross functional team, and Elena accepted without comment as her calendar filled, meetings stacked, calls ran late, and people praised her reliability while treating it as a resource they could spend.

On Thursday evening a senior executive invited Elena to drinks with a client framed as exposure, opportunity, relationship building, and Elena went. The client spoke loudly and asked personal questions, Elena answering plainly without deflecting or protecting herself, and she did not notice the shift in the conversation until the executive placed a hand on her shoulder to guide her toward a quieter corner. The touch was casual and unnecessary, and when Elena looked at the hand and then the executive's face, he told her she was doing great, unflappable, rare, while the client leaned in and said she was tough and could handle anything. Elena heard the words and felt nothing that would initiate refusal, and when the executive asked if she could stay back after the client left, he said it like a request and a compliment, and Elena stayed.

They spoke about her future, promotion, how the organisation rewarded people who did not create problems, and the executives' tone softened into familiarity as the room became smaller. At one point he asked whether Elena wanted to come back to his hotel lobby to continue the discussion, and Elena paused, not fear but processing, searching for a reason to refuse as consequences appeared faster than preference. She said it was late, he agreed and said they could keep it professional, and Elena nodded and went.

In the lobby they spoke for twenty minutes, then the executive produced a short confidentiality statement, saying it was standard for client-related conversations. Elena signed and he thanked her, not touching her again and not doing anything overt, simply watching her accept each step without resistance.

When Elena returned home, she stood in her bathroom and looked at her face, no redness, no tension, no shame, and tried to decide whether anything had been wrong. Nothing had happened that could be named as harm, and that was the problem.

The next day her colleague asked how the client dinner went and Elena said fine. The colleague said Elena looked tired and Elena answered that she worked late, but the colleague said that wasn't what she meant, then asked whether Elena ever said no anymore. Elena answered that no wasn't required if the outcome was correct, and the colleague asked correct for who, and Elena did not answer.

That weekend Elena visited her sister again and her sister watched her quietly while Elena cleaned the kitchen, moving efficiently without stopping or resting. Her sister said Elena didn't slow down, Elena answering there was no need, and her sister put a hand on Elena's arm and asked whether Elena felt anything when she did that. Elena said she did, that she noticed it, and when her sister asked whether Elena liked it Elena searched for urgency and preference and found neither, replying that it was fine. Her sister let go.

Later, alone in the guest room, Elena tried to remember what her body had once done when it wanted to leave, the tightening, the heat, the impulse to move away, recalling the facts but not the force.

On Monday morning another insurance message arrived, clearer, informing her that recovery status had been updated and that ongoing coverage assumed continued compliance with recommended maintenance, that nonparticipation might affect eligibility. Elena read it twice and forwarded it to the company liaison asking if anything was required, and the liaison replied within minutes, saying all good and keeping doing what she was doing. Elena returned to work.

At her next follow up with Dr. Nile, Elena arrived straight from the office, sat down, and answered questions quickly while Jax watched her more closely. Jax asked how many hours Elena worked last week, Elena answering a lot, more than usual, and when Jax asked if Elena wanted to Elena said it was required. Jax pressed her to answer the question, and Elena said it made sense because the project needed it. Jax asked whether Elena noticed fatigue and Elena confirmed she did, then Jax asked what Elena did when she noticed it and Elena said she continued, and when Jax asked why Elena said it was manageable.

Jax leaned forward and asked what would make it unmanageable, and Elena hesitated long enough to admit she didn't know, and Jax wrote something down.

"We're going to do a simple exercise," Jax said. "I will ask you for something, you will refuse, not because you need to, because you can."

Elena looked uncertain and asked refuse what, and Jax told her anything, starting small, asking Elena to stay an extra hour after the appointment and to say no. Elena opened her mouth, closed it, then said no finally, the word sounding unfamiliar like a language she had not spoken in a long time. Jax asked her to say it again and Elena repeated it faster, and when Jax asked what Elena felt when she said it Elena searched herself and said nothing, it was just a word.

"That is the point," Jax said quietly. "It should not be just a word."

Elena frowned and said no caused problems. Jax told her it only caused problems in systems that benefited from compliance, and Elena looked away as the sentence landed as concept rather than threat.

Jax asked how Elena knew when she was consenting, and Elena replied when something happened, and Jax corrected her that it was compliance, not consent. Elena looked confused and said it worked, asking why she would resist something that worked, and the question was sincere. Jax ended the assessment early.

In the corridor outside the room Jax stopped and replayed the interaction, Elena not distressed and not impaired, functioning, her metrics excellent, and that was the problem.

Back at work Elena travelled the following week, fixed the issue, worked long hours, received praise, and the executive emailed thanks for stepping up. The insurance liaison contacted her again requesting confirmation that she remained stable under travel and high workload, and Elena completed the form within ten minutes. That night in the hotel room she stood at the window and tried to remember what fear had felt like, recalling facts, places, reasons, while the sensation itself stayed inaccessible, and she did not panic or mourn, noting the absence and moving on.

In the following month Elena's protections began to disappear, flexibility removed, work assigned by default, accommodations erased as her file was marked fully restored. The insurance forms became more explicit, recovery compliance required ongoing participation, any deviation might affect coverage and employment suitability, polite language with a clear condition, and Elena read each notice and responded, confirming, agreeing, acknowledging. She did not ask why the forms kept coming and did not ask what would happen if she stopped answering.

At a team meeting a junior colleague joked that Elena was the department's stabilizer, someone calling her the insurance policy, the room laughing while Elena smiled lightly because it was expected. After the meeting, the colleague who had warned her earlier approached again and asked whether Elena even cared whether she cared about them taking everything and about never pushing back, and Elena asked what she meant by everything. The colleague said boundaries, time, self, and Elena answered that pushing back didn't change outcomes, and the colleague said it changed you, and Elena returned to her desk.

That evening, in Jax's office, Elena's file remained open on the screen, improvement sustained, function expanded, no adverse indicators, and Jax added a private note not visible to the dashboard.

Compliance increasing without distress. Boundary recognition delayed. Refusal latency rising. Monitor for reuse risk. Audit external forms.

She saved it and sat back as the system continued to reward Elena and Elena continued to absorb, neither of them naming what had been lost because there was no code for it, no field for it, no box to tick. Function had returned. Free-will had not.

Chapter Five

Cleared for Duty

om woke before the alarm because he always did, a habit that
had survived deployments, injuries, and long stretches of
civilian time that were meant to soften it out of him but never
did. He lay still and listened. The room was quiet, too quiet, and in the
past quiet had been the moment before impact, the space where his
body prepared for something it could not yet see, but now it was just
quiet.

He waited for tension to rise, the pulse in the neck, the tightening
behind the eyes, the scan of exits that ran before thought, and nothing
came. When he sat up his heart rate stayed level and his breathing
stayed even, and the absence registered as clarity, as progress, at least
that was what he told himself.

In the kitchen Tom made coffee and drank it standing while
checking his phone, a message from his unit liaison, a calendar
reminder, and a note from his insurer confirming receipt of his latest
assessment. He opened the message and read it once.

Clearance review scheduled. Preliminary indicators positive.

He nodded once, as if someone were watching.

Tom had been operational once, and that was the word they used,
operational, meaning he functioned inside chaos without fragmenting,

meaning he could act while others froze, meaning he carried things most people could not. After the incident the word changed to unfit, and the diagnosis arrived with clinical precision, post-traumatic stress, persistent hypervigilance, impaired threat modulation, the symptoms described cleanly as if naming them contained them.

For two years he lived between therapies, exposure, medication, simulations that left him shaking, and he learned the language of recovery the way you learned a drill. He learned how to describe progress without believing it. Then came the referral, framed as optional, experimental, conservative, and he was told it would not erase memory, only intensity.

Tom did not care about intensity. He cared about readiness.

In the operating room before sedation Jax asked the questions she asked everyone, whether he understood she would stop early, whether he understood more relief was possible than she would provide, whether he understood he could refuse at any point, and he answered each one the same way, short and correct. He understood refusal conceptually and did not believe he would use it.

After the procedure, the world felt quieter, not numb and not dull, less urgent. The difference showed up first in training. Tom returned to the range under observation and the noise did not trigger the familiar spike, his hands stayed steady, his focus sharpened, and instructors watched closely as if waiting for the old instability to reassert itself.

"Looks good," one of them said.

Tom nodded.

He did feel good, and that was new, not happiness, not relief, readiness. He slept through the night and stopped waking with images that did not belong to the present, stopped scanning crowds, stopped counting exits, stopped doing arithmetic in his head before crossing a room. He passed every assessment, and the clearance process came in layers, medical, psychological, functional, each stage ending with the same notation.

Improved.

When the insurance representative called her tone was congratulatory, telling him his response exceeded expectations and that they were seeing sustained functional recovery. Tom thanked her because gratitude felt appropriate, and she explained next steps, updated coverage classification, adjusted premiums, a pathway back to operational status.

"Your treatment has restored capacity," she said.

The word capacity landed cleanly because it sounded official, and she sent forms. Tom completed them immediately, confirming he felt capable of returning to duty, denying hesitation in high stress environments, consenting to future assessments if required, and he did not consider the alternative because the alternative did not look like choice, it looked like failure.

The first redeployment briefing took place in a windowless room with maps on screens, familiar language, familiar posture, and Tom listened without tension, absorbing details efficiently. When asked questions he answered clearly, and his commanding officer studied him before saying he was steady, then adding that he was better than before. Tom did not correct him.

After the briefing, the unit medic pulled Tom aside and asked how he really was, and Tom considered before answering that he was fine. She told him that wasn't an answer and Tom said it was accurate, and she watched him closely, reminding him he was cleared but not invulnerable, telling him to report anything that felt off. Tom agreed, the words coming with automatic discipline, not preference, and that automaticness did not worry him yet.

In the days before deployment Tom trained harder, longer hours, more drills, and his endurance surprised even him. Fatigue registered as information rather than warning. At home, his partner noticed the change, telling him he didn't jump anymore, and Tom confirmed it. She asked if that was good, and Tom said it was, then she said he didn't get angry either. Tom frowned and said he didn't need to, remembering how anger used to sit close to the surface, frightening her and frightening him, and now it was absent.

She touched his arm and asked if he still felt things. Tom considered and said he felt clear. She smiled uncertainly and said that wasn't the same thing, and Tom did not respond because he did not have a response that stayed inside his new vocabulary.

The deployment was shorter than previous ones, contained, controlled, and the environment was volatile but predictable. Tom performed well, following orders precisely and taking initiative when required, not hesitating, not freezing, moving through tasks as if hesitation had been replaced by a clean line from instruction to action.

During one operation a civilian moved unexpectedly into the line of action. Before, the moment would have triggered a surge of adrenaline and a split second of internal conflict, the body arguing with the mind. This time Tom assessed and acted without delay, adjusted position, neutralized the threat, no error. Afterward his commanding officer clapped him on the shoulder and called it clean, and Tom nodded.

That night lying in his bunk Tom waited for the delayed response, the replay, the tremor, the guilt, and nothing came. He slept.

The next operation was riskier, closer quarters, uncertain intel, the kind of situation that used to produce hesitation, and Tom moved through it with precision. Afterward a junior member approached and asked how Tom stayed so calm, and Tom considered before saying he didn't think about it. The man called it the trick, and Tom did not reply because it did not feel like a trick, it felt like a missing step.

Midway through deployment an insurance review request arrived via secure channel, routine performance confirmation. Tom completed the assessment between operations, denying distress after engagement and denying reservations about continuing operational duty, and the answers felt accurate. The review was approved within hours.

The second week brought an incident, an unexpected escalation, a miscommunication, a civilian injured. Tom acted quickly, contained the situation, followed protocol, did everything right. Afterward the injured civilian cried loudly and desperately, and Tom watched without reaction. A teammate noticed and asked if he was okay, and Tom said he was. The teammate hesitated and said Tom didn't even flinch, and Tom replied there was nothing to flinch at. The teammate said nothing.

Back at base the medic requested a check-in, telling him he was doing well but something was different, that he wasn't processing the same way. Tom said he didn't need to. She frowned and said that wasn't how it worked, and Tom told her it did for him. She noted something in his file, the gesture quiet and procedural, the kind of note that mattered later.

At the end of the deployment Tom received commendation and his clearance status was reaffirmed. The insurance representative called again, praising excellent outcomes and saying his response validated the intervention. Tom thanked her, and she added that his coverage remained optimal, and that continued participation was assumed. Tom agreed without thinking about the weight of the assumption.

When he returned home his partner hugged him tightly and said he was back. Tom confirmed it, and when she pulled back, she studied his face and said he was different. Tom told her he was better. She hesitated and said he didn't seem shaken by anything, and Tom replied there was nothing to be shaken by. She told him that wasn't true. Tom did not argue.

Weeks passed. Tom remained operational, assignments continued, performance stayed exemplary, and the system responded accordingly. Premiums dropped, clearance level increased, suitability rating updated. Suitability appeared repeatedly in his file like an anchor word, not a compliment, a classification.

At his next follow up with Jax, Tom sat upright across from her, calm and controlled. Jax asked how he had been and Tom said good, then she asked about distress, hesitation, and resistance. Tom denied each one until she asked about resistance to orders, to situations, to things he did not want to do. Tom paused and asked resistance to what. Jax clarified, and Tom considered before saying he didn't see the point, and Jax's pen stopped.

She asked whether he ever wanted to stop. Tom answered that he stopped if stopping was required. Jax told him it was not the question, and Tom searched for a cleaner response before saying he didn't want to stop. Jax leaned back slightly and asked why, and Tom said because he functioned, that this was what functioning looked like. Jax asked function for whom, and Tom said for the role. When she asked and for him, Tom paused long enough to admit he didn't think it mattered. Jax noted the response without comment.

Later that day an audit request arrived, not from insurance directly but from an oversight body, routine outcome verification. Tom was not concerned. He completed forms, attended interviews, answered questions clearly, consenting to redeployment, denying pressure, affirming that he could refuse. No one asked him when he last had.

On his next deployment the risk was higher, intel uncertain, margin for error thinner, and Tom acted decisively, following orders, not hesitating. The mission succeeded, and afterward his commanding officer said quietly that Tom didn't hesitate anymore and that it was useful.

Useful.

Tom nodded.

That night lying in his bunk Tom tried to remember what fear had felt like, recalling the situations, the stakes, the consequences, while the sensation itself stayed inaccessible. He did not panic and did not mourn. He slept.

Back home his partner grew uneasy, telling him he didn't argue anymore and Tom replied there was nothing to argue about. She said that wasn't true, and Tom told her to say what she wanted. She opened her mouth then closed it, then told him he used to push back. Tom searched for the memory and called it inefficient. She stared at him and said he sounded like a report. Tom did not respond.

The insurance forms continued, each one framing his condition as resolved, each one reinforcing the expectation of continued participation, and when a form stated that coverage assumed availability for operational duty Tom signed without comment.

At his next appointment Jax asked him to refuse something deliberately, telling him to say no, not because he needed to, because he could. Tom asked no to what, and Jax asked him to stay longer that day and to refuse. Tom opened his mouth, closed it, then said no. The word felt flat, unloaded, and when Jax asked what he felt Tom said nothing.

"That's not neutrality," Jax said quietly. "That's erosion."

Tom frowned and asked erosion of what.

"Of choice," Jax said.

Tom did not understand the concern, not yet, because he still believed that clear action was the same thing as freedom.

Outside her office Jax reviewed his file. Performance optimal. Distress absent. Compliance complete. She added a private note.

Operational reuse risk confirmed. Absence of refusal. Monitor redeployment pressure. Cross check insurer triggers.

She saved it. The system continued to reward Tom and Tom continued to serve, function replacing hesitation, utility replacing choice, and neither of them could yet name the cost because the cost did not show up as a symptom, it showed up as silence where an argument used to be.

Chapter Six

The Perfect Witness

Maya had learned how to tell the story, and that was the first thing people noticed. She did not rush, she did not ramble, she did not cry at the wrong moments, and she knew where to pause and where to continue because she had practiced enough times that the shape of the narrative no longer surprised her, it arrived in order, controlled and repeatable. When she spoke, people leaned forward, and that had not always been true.

Before the incident Maya had been careful but not controlled. She spoke quickly and second guessed herself, apologized when she did not need to, and her voice carried uncertainty even when her words were correct. After the incident uncertainty became a liability, and the system made that clear in a way no one needed to say directly. Lawyers told her gently, judges told her indirectly, outcomes told her without words. When she cried in the first interview the officer nodded sympathetically but did not write much down, when she hesitated the questions sharpened, when she corrected herself, the room cooled. Later, when she learned to speak cleanly, everything changed.

The referral to Dr. Nile came through her insurer. The language was careful, optional, supportive, framed as stabilizing trauma responses to improve testimony reliability, and reliability was the word that mattered. The procedure was described as conservative, it would not erase memory, it would reduce intensity, it would help her remain present without distress. Maya agreed immediately, not framing it as healing, framing it as preparation.

In the operating room, before sedation, Dr. Nile asked the questions she asked everyone, whether Maya understood the procedure would stop short of full relief, whether Maya understood she could refuse at any point, whether Maya understood this would not make her stronger. Maya answered in short confirmations, precise and compliant, because she had learned that precision was safer than nuance.

After the procedure Maya noticed the change almost immediately. The images remained, the facts remained, the sequence of events stayed intact, and the reaction was gone. When she replayed the memory, it felt distant, like a report she had read rather than something she had lived, and that distance felt like control, like competence, like something she could use.

In the weeks that followed her legal team noticed the difference. After a mock examination one of them said she was solid, no emotional volatility, very credible, and Maya heard the word credible and felt relief. She returned to court and when she took the stand she did not tremble, did not avert her eyes, did not apologize for taking time to answer. She described what happened in precise language, dates, locations, actions, outcomes, and when the defence attempted to provoke her, she did not react. She corrected them calmly and waited for the question to finish before answering. The judge nodded and the jury listened.

Afterward her lawyer squeezed her hand and told her it was excellent. Maya did not feel proud. She felt complete, as if she had delivered what the process required and nothing more had been demanded of her. Outside the courtroom reporters asked questions and Maya answered evenly, and when one said she seemed very composed Maya confirmed it with a simple statement. Her words were quoted the next day, and a headline framed her as strength, victim shows strength in testimony, strength becoming the story the system preferred to tell because it was clean and flattering and easy to file.

The prosecutor asked if Maya would speak publicly, educational forums, advocacy groups, and survivor networks. Maya agreed, the response arrived easily, and before the incident public speaking would have caused panic, but now it felt procedural, a role she could perform without paying the old cost.

At her next follow up Dr. Nile asked about court and Maya said it went well, and when Jax asked how it felt Maya said clear. Jax asked whether anything unsettled her and Maya said no. Jax asked whether she felt pressure to perform and Maya paused before saying it was expected and that she met the expectation, and Jax told her that was not the same thing. Maya did not understand the distinction, because expectation and survival had merged in her mind long ago, and now the separation felt theoretical.

In the weeks that followed Maya became the example. Her insurer reduced premiums. Her legal team cited composure in filings. Advocacy groups invited her to speak. She accepted every invitation, and when asked why she said the same thing each time, if it helps, the phrase correct and unexamined, virtue shaped like a justification.

At one forum a woman approached her afterward and asked how she stayed so calm. Maya considered and said she did not engage emotionally. The woman said that sounded hard and Maya replied that it was efficient, the word surprising even her when it landed, efficient.

The legal system responded as if she had discovered a cheating code. Judges praised her clarity, prosecutors relied on her steadiness, defence counsel struggled to destabilize her. In one cross examination the defence suggested her memory was unreliable due to trauma and Maya responded calmly, explaining that the events were intact and only her reaction had changed. The attorney asked whether she felt distress when recalling the event and Maya said she did not, and when asked if she considered that normal, she nodded and said it worked. The moment hung, not because anyone objected, but because no one did. The jury watched closely and the process kept moving.

After the verdict Maya was congratulated repeatedly, people telling her she was strong and that she did not let it break her. Maya nodded and did not correct them because the correction would have required a different language, a language for costs that did not show up as symptoms. In private she noticed changes she could not articulate. She stopped flinching when people stood too close, stopped noticing when conversations crossed boundaries, stopped leaving rooms when she felt uncomfortable, and the sensation that once prompted withdrawal no longer arrived.

At a networking event organized by an advocacy group a senior donor placed a hand on her back while speaking. Maya registered the contact and did not react. The donor leaned closer and told her she was remarkable, so composed, and Maya nodded. The interaction ended without incident, nothing overt happened, nothing that could be named as harm, and later when she replayed the moment, she noted the absence of reaction. She did not feel relief and did not feel concern. She moved on.

Her insurer contacted her again with a notice, based on sustained recovery and functional stability, certain accommodations were no longer applicable, framed as positive. Maya read it and accepted it because the notice carried the tone of reward, and reward had always come with conditions even when no one said so.

Her legal team encouraged further advocacy work, paid engagements, consulting roles for training legal professionals. Her lawyer told her she had credibility and people listened, and Maya agreed again, an uncomplicated assent that felt like motion rather than decision. The engagements increased and at each one Maya told the story cleanly, without visible distress, without deviation, and the audience responded with admiration, calling her an inspiration. Maya nodded because the script was familiar, the role was functional.

In one session a facilitator asked how Maya learned to regulate her emotions so effectively. Maya paused and said she did not regulate them, they did not arise. The room went quiet and the facilitator smiled tightly, labelling it resilience, and Maya accepted the label because labels were how systems closed files.

At her next appointment Dr. Nile asked Maya to describe a recent boundary crossing. Maya searched her memory and described a man at an event who stood too close. Jax asked what Maya did and Maya said nothing, explaining it was not necessary. Jax asked whether Maya wanted him to move and Maya paused longer this time, then said she did not think about it that way. Jax asked her to think about it now and Maya admitted she would have preferred more space, and when asked whether she expressed that Maya said she did not, explaining it did not affect the outcome. Jax wrote something down and did not argue, as if arguing would only teach the system how to hide better.

Later that week Maya was asked to review training materials for investigators and her feedback was praised for clarity and neutrality. A coordinator told her she removed emotion from the process, and it helped everyone focus on facts. Maya nodded and began to notice how often neutrality was rewarded. When she spoke without emotion doors opened, when she stayed composed people trusted her, and emotionless credibility became currency she did not remember choosing to earn.

At a private dinner with donors Maya was seated beside a senior legal figure who spoke about reform and efficiency and how trauma victims complicated proceedings. He told Maya she was different and did not make it messy, then called her ideal, saying if more witnesses were like her cases would move faster. The comment was praise and Maya treated it as such, nodding because the process rewarded the absence of disruption.

Later that night she stood in her bathroom and tried to remember what fear had felt like. She could recall the facts of the incident, the sequence, the harm, and the sensation itself stayed inaccessible. She did not panic and did not grieve. She noted the absence and moved on, as if note and move on were the only two verbs still available.

At her next follow up Dr. Nile asked a different question, whether Maya felt pressure to remain this way. Maya frowned and asked remain what way, and when Jax said composed Maya considered before saying people expected it. Jax asked what would happen if she were not and Maya paused longer, admitting they would be disappointed, and Jax named it as pressure. Maya did not respond because the naming did not restore the sensation, it only clarified the shape.

Jax asked whether Maya could withdraw consent for public speaking. "Yes," Maya said quickly and confidently. "Have you?" Jax dug further. "No," was Maya's unsurprising reply. When asked why, Maya hesitated and admitted it would disrupt things. Jax asked what process and Maya answered the process, as if the process were a person that could be harmed. Jax's pen stopped.

After the appointment Maya received another insurance notice, continued coverage contingent on participation in recommended recovery activities, and public advocacy was listed as beneficial. Maya read it carefully and the word contingent did not alarm her, it clarified expectations, and she continued participating.

At a conference Maya delivered a keynote, speaking calmly about the incident, the process, and the importance of resilience. The audience stood to applaud, and someone told her she was proof that trauma did not define her. Maya nodded. In the hotel lobby an organizer approached and asked her to be on a panel tomorrow, short notice, and Maya agreed again. He smiled and said she never said no. Maya registered the phrase and it felt factual rather than flattering, a pattern spoken aloud.

Later alone in her room Maya tried to decide whether she wanted to be on the panel, and the concept of wanting felt abstract, preference without urgency, thought without force. She attended the panel anyway.

The system continued to reward her. In Jax's office Maya's file remained open, outcome sustained, distress absent, credibility increased. Jax added a private note.

Testimonial reliability improved. Emotional flattening evident. Consent framed as efficiency. Monitor for institutional dependence.

She saved it. The system continued to praise Maya and Maya continued to perform, and neither of them named what had been lost because the loss was not disruptive, it was useful. The legal system moved faster, cases closed cleanly, Maya became the standard, and function had returned while consent thinned, not in a single breach, in a thousand approvals that no longer felt like choices.

Chapter Seven

Protected

T he first sign was not a demand, it was a correction, and Jax noticed it while reviewing a draft protocol circulated for internal comment. Her language had been retained but repositioned, consent still present but no longer anchoring the document, reduced to a subsection, a condition rather than a premise. She scrolled back up and read the executive summary again, outcomes leading the page, stability, reduced volatility, sustained participation, participation in what remains undefined.

She added comments in the margin, direct and unambiguous. Consent is prerequisite, not modifier. Refusal must remain structurally protected. Treatment cannot be framed as enabling productivity. She saved and closed the document, expecting at minimum a negotiation, and two hours later the revised version returned. Her comments were acknowledged and none were implemented, and instead a note sat beneath the executive summary, clinical nuance to be addressed in implementation phase. Jax stared at the sentence longer than necessary because implementation was where nuance went to die, and the phrasing was familiar, the kind that preserved tone while burying substance.

That afternoon an administrator she had not met requested a meeting. The email was brief, alignment discussion, short notice, and Jax accepted. The meeting room was smaller than usual, no glass walls, no water poured in advance, and three people waited when she arrived. She recognized none of them, and the introductions were efficient, titles blurring into function, policy, risk liaison, external affairs, external being the only word that mattered.

They thanked her for leadership and praised her restraint, repeating her own language back to her with a care that felt rehearsed. Then they spoke about exposure, not hers, they clarified, the institutions, and one of them said innovation attracts attention, attention attracts scrutiny. Jax replied that scrutiny was appropriate, and the man agreed before adding that unmanaged scrutiny can distort perception, the warning wrapped as concern.

They spoke about messaging, about how her work was being discussed outside the hospital, in policy forums, insurance reviews, regulatory briefings she had not attended. A woman said they wanted to make sure her intent was preserved. Jax asked by whom, and the man replied smoothly that it would be preserved by them, on her behalf. Jax said evenly that she did not require representation, and the woman replied that she already had it, whether she wanted it or not. Silence settled, not hostile, procedural, the silence of decisions already taken.

They slid a document across the table. It was not a contract, it was a communications framework, approved language, approved descriptors, phrases to avoid. One phrase was highlighted, treatment as prerequisite. Jax tapped the line. This should not exist, she said. The man answered that it existed because others were using it and they were containing it. Jax said they were normalizing it. The woman corrected that they were contextualizing it. Jax closed the document because the correction was the point, replacing refusal with semantics.

This is not my work, she said. No, the man agreed, it is the work around your work. Jax stood and told them it should not involve her, and the woman smiled tightly and said it already did. Jax left without closing the distance, letting the meeting end on their line, not hers.

That evening she reviewed patient files again. Nothing had changed clinically, and that was the problem because the changes were happening elsewhere, in templates, in summaries, in the language people would quote when they wanted to move a boundary. Two days later a journalist emailed her office, polite, requesting comment on a story about breakthrough trauma interventions reducing long term insurance burden. Jax did not respond, and the story ran anyway. Her name appeared once, quoted indirectly, framed as cautious, ethical, a responsible innovator, flattering and inaccurate, a soft portrait designed to make resistance look unreasonable.

The next morning Marcus called and asked if she had seen the coverage. Jax said she had, and Marcus told her they were moving faster than expected. Jax said they were moving without her, and Marcus paused before saying that was why he was calling. They met that afternoon, and this time Marcus did not choose a neutral location, he chose his office. The space was understated, no branding, no visible affiliation, files organized by function not client, and the absence was deliberate.

They're insulating you, Marcus said, and themselves. By rewriting my intent, Jax replied. By controlling narrative before regulation arrives, Marcus said. Jax called it capture, not protection, and Marcus agreed without hesitation, saying it escalates. He pulled up a briefing note on his screen, internal, distribution limited. Projected impact of trauma capacity restoration on claims duration. Jax scanned it and said they were already modelling this as baseline. Marcus said yes, and added that deviation would look like regression. Or resistance, Jax said, and Marcus nodded because that was the intended translation.

Jax looked at him sharply and reminded him he said he would shield her. Marcus said he was, and that this was what shielding looked like early. Jax asked if shielding meant letting them proceed, and Marcus replied that it meant slowing how they proceeded. He said they wanted to formalize prerequisites, and he had pushed it into pilot language, voluntary adoption, and review gates. Jax asked about consent and Marcus met her gaze and said he kept it explicit. Jax said for now, and Marcus did not deny it.

They're testing boundaries, Marcus said, your boundaries and mine. Jax asked what happens when they cross them, and Marcus leaned back slightly and said then it becomes visible. Jax asked visible to whom and Marcus said regulators, boards, people who cared about exposure more than outcomes. Jax said that meant letting harm occur, and Marcus kept his voice calm and said it meant documenting attempts, because systems only confessed when paper forced them to.

Jax stood and said she did not agree to be a case study. Marcus looked up and said she already was, and that the question was whether she would be silent or structured. Jax turned away and looked out at the city, clean movement, efficient systems, and she thought of Elena, Tom, Maya, and how none of them would complain. That was the leverage, the quiet that made pressure safe to apply. She turned back and told Marcus that if they forced prerequisites, she would shut it down. Marcus nodded once and said he would make sure the shutdown costs them. It was the first time he spoke in terms of cost, not intent.

Jax told him that was not protection, it was retaliation. Marcus replied quietly that in systems they were the same thing. Jax left without agreeing to anything, and she hated that this was now the language, not medicine but containment.

That night an internal memo circulated. Subject, Interim Guidance Update. Language softened, consent emphasized, no prerequisites stated, for now. Jax read it once and understood it as cover, not surrender, the cover holding, barely.

The first call came from someone who did not introduce themselves as insurance, because they never did. The voicemail was polite and professional, referencing alignment concerns and requesting a brief discussion about clinical thresholds in applied contexts. Jax deleted it without listening twice. The second call came the next morning, same number, same tone, and a follow-up email arrived minutes later. Subject, Clarification Request. The body thanked her for leadership, acknowledged the complexity of innovation in sensitive domains, then outlined a hypothetical scenario. If a patient declined treatment after referral and adverse outcomes followed, how would responsibility be assessed? Jax read the sentence three times because it was not a question, it was a framing exercise designed to make refusal look negligent.

She forwarded it to Marcus with a single line. They're testing liability. Marcus replied within minutes. Yes. And they're doing it badly. I'll handle this.

By midday hospital administration requested an urgent meeting and the tone was different, less collaborative, more procedural. When Jax arrived the room was full, operations, risk, legal, external affairs, and someone she did not recognize who did not speak. They did not thank her this time. They spoke about exposure, reputational risk, how innovation carried obligations beyond clinical intent, and one of them used the phrase foreseeable harm.

Jax leaned forward and said foreseeable harm occurs when coercion is applied, not when consent is preserved. The legal representative nodded and said that was precisely what they needed to clarify. Clarify meant narrow, and they presented a revised guidance note. Treatment remained voluntary, but refusal now triggered additional steps, secondary assessment, documentation, and notification to external stakeholders. A risk officer said it was not a prerequisite; it was a safeguard. Jax said it was friction applied to refusal. The legal representative called it accountability. Jax asked for whom, and he answered for the system.

Jax closed the document and said it creates pressure to comply. The risk officer said it creates transparency, and transparency sounded like coercion with better language. Before Jax could respond, the silent man spoke for the first time. He said they were not asking her to change her clinical thresholds, they were asking her to acknowledge the downstream impact of refusal. Jax asked what happens if she does not, and the man's expression stayed neutral as he said then others will.

Jax stood and ended the meeting. Outside the room Marcus was waiting. He had not been invited, and that itself was information. He said it was faster than expected. Jax said they were escalating. Marcus agreed and said that meant they were exposed. He walked with her down the corridor and said they pushed liability framing too early, which was good. Jax said it was not good because patients would feel it. Marcus stopped and said it meant they were impatient, and impatience leaves a trail.

They went to his office. Marcus pulled up documents Jax had not seen, internal memos, modelling notes, draft policy language circulated between insurers, and the throughline was unmistakable, recovery as obligation, treatment as expectation, refusal as risk signal. Jax said they were coordinating. Marcus said yes, but not aligned. He highlighted a section, disagreement between carriers regarding enforceability of treatment-linked coverage. Marcus said they did not agree on how far they could push, and none wanted to be first to be named. Jax said so they push quietly. Marcus corrected that they push indirectly, through hospitals, through protocols that look neutral, through clinicians made responsible for the downstream.

Jax sat down and said she would not allow it. Marcus said he knew and that was why he stepped in. He opened another file, a formal objection lodged with the consortium's governance committee, authored by him, filed that morning. Grounds, regulatory exposure, consent erosion, litigation risk associated with implied coercion. Marcus said they cannot ignore this, it triggers review. Jax said and retaliation. Marcus said yes, on him, without drama, stating cost like weather.

Jax asked what he gave them, and Marcus hesitated briefly before saying he gave them a slower path, pilot framing, narrow cohort, explicit consent language written into funding agreements. Jax asked what he gave in exchange, and Marcus met her gaze and said he tied his name to it. Jax called it sacrifice. Marcus shrugged and said it buys time. Jax did not ask what time for because she already knew. Time for thresholds to hold while the system learned how to press them.

They'll come back, Jax said. Marcus agreed, but said next time it would be through process, not pressure. That afternoon the guidance note was revised again. The additional steps attached to refusal were removed, language softened, consent re-centered. An internal memo followed. Subject, Interim Pause on Expanded Application. Marcus forwarded it to Jax with a single line. This is as far as they'll retreat.

That evening Jax reviewed patient files again. No changes, no new requirements, for now. She called Elena for a routine check-in and Elena answered immediately. Jax asked if everything was okay and

Elena said it was. Jax asked about changes in coverage and Elena said no, everything looks good. Jax ended the call and dialed Tom. He answered from a training facility, all good, nothing unusual, his voice the same tone he used for status updates. Maya was harder to reach and when she answered she sounded distracted. They asked me to update my participation plan, she said, and she added that it was optional. Optional, Jax repeated. Maya confirmed it and said it helps keep the file clean. Jax closed her eyes briefly because clean was the word that always preceded pressure.

The cover was holding, barely.

The next week a meeting was scheduled with the consortium's oversight committee and Marcus attended alone. He reported back that evening, saying they were backing off publicly and privately furious. Jax asked what that meant and Marcus said it meant they would wait, then look for variance. Jax asked what happens if they find it, and Marcus said then she becomes the problem. Jax nodded because she had expected that, and expectations were not comfort, only clarity.

She asked Marcus if he regretted stepping in and he shook his head and said no, this is the job. Jax said this is not a job, this is my work. Marcus met her gaze and said that's why I care. It was the first time the statement felt personal, even though it was still framed professionally, and for a moment Jax allowed herself to believe him, to believe that the system could be managed, that thresholds could be defended, that harm could be limited through vigilance. The belief would not last, but for now the cover held.

Chapter Eight

Fit for Purpose

The language changed quietly. Jax noticed it first in a briefing note circulated without attribution, no announcement, no cover email, just an updated attachment nested in a thread she was already part of. She read it once, then again, and the substitution was clean enough to look accidental.

The term treatment had been replaced everywhere it mattered. Capacity restoration. The phrase appeared repeatedly, embedded in sentences that read professional, unremarkable, built to sound like administrative hygiene instead of ideological shift. Capacity restoration enables individuals to resume functional participation. Capacity restoration reduces long-term dependency. Capacity restoration supports system sustainability.

Jax scrolled back to the header. Interim Classification Update. Interim was doing a lot of work, and she could feel the weight behind it, the word designed to soothe the moment while the structure hardened beneath it. She forwarded the document to Marcus with a single line. They're changing the ontology.

His reply came quickly. Yes. And once they do, consent becomes implied. Jax closed the file and stood, the decision settling in her body before it reached language. In the corridor outside her office, staff moved efficiently, clinicians, administrators, researchers, everyone working within frameworks they did not design and rarely questioned. She thought of Elena, Tom, Maya. None of them would read this document, and none of them would be asked to.

The classification meeting took place a week later. Jax was invited this time, and so was Marcus, and the invitation itself felt like proof that the decision had moved beyond her. The room was larger than usual, glass walls, neutral lighting, a deliberate transparency meant to signal that nothing improper could occur inside it. Representatives from multiple insurers attended remotely, their screens lining one wall, faces arranged in neat rows, titles listed beneath names like credentials and warnings.

A facilitator opened the session. "We're here to align on terminology," she said, "to ensure consistency across systems." Consistency was the stated goal, always the stated goal, and Jax listened as slides appeared, graphs, outcome curves, utilisation models, each one clean enough to make coercion look like mathematics. The language was careful. No one said prerequisite. No one said coercion. Instead, they spoke of eligibility optimisation, functional readiness, risk mitigation, terms designed to preserve distance from the human subject.

One slide displayed a comparison. Pre-intervention trajectory versus post-intervention capacity. The post-intervention line rose smoothly, too smoothly, and the absence of variance read like a sales pitch. "By reframing this as capacity restoration," one of the insurers said, "we remove stigma."

"You remove choice," Jax said.

The room went still, and the facilitator smiled politely as if this were a tone problem. "Choice remains," she said. "But context matters." Jax asked what context, and another insurer answered without blinking. "The context of risk. If capacity can be restored, declining it carries implications." Jax asked for whom, and he replied, "For the system."

Marcus leaned forward slightly. "That assumes neutrality," he said, "which this is not." The insurer nodded, almost pleased. "Nothing is neutral," he said. "That's why classification matters." Jax spoke carefully, keeping her voice level because anger would be filed as instability. "My work does not restore capacity," she said. "It reduces interference. There is a difference." The facilitator nodded. "Clinically, yes. Administratively, the outcome is what matters."

Outcome over intent. Jax felt the shift settle, not as argument but as infrastructure. Once the term capacity entered the frame, everything downstream changed. Capacity could be measured, benchmarked, required. Trauma could not, which meant trauma could be erased from the language without ever being denied. The meeting ended with no vote and no resolution, and that was the resolution.

Two days later the updated classification appeared in internal systems. Capacity Restoration Program. Her name was listed as clinical lead. She had not agreed to that title, and she knew that agreement was no longer part of the mechanism. She called Marcus. "They did it anyway."

"Yes," Marcus replied. "They always do."

"Can you undo it?"

"I can slow its application," he said. "I can't reverse classification once it's live."

Jax asked what slowing looked like, already hearing the answer. "Pilot language. Limited cohorts. Review checkpoints." She asked about consent, and Marcus hesitated just long enough to be honest. "Consent becomes procedural," he said, "not central."

Jax closed her eyes. Procedural consent was not consent, it was documentation, and documentation was how systems converted moral questions into completed fields. The first effect appeared in Elena's file, a routine update, automated. Coverage status adjusted. Capacity restored. Accommodation review scheduled. Elena did not call to ask about it. She accepted the update as confirmation of progress, as a stamp of improvement she did not have to interpret.

Tom's clearance documentation changed next. Capacity fully restored. Suitability reaffirmed. No limitations noted. Maya's advocacy engagements were reclassified as functional participation, the phrase appearing in a funding note as if it were a neutral description. Public testimony supports systemic efficiency. Jax stared at the sentence until it blurred, then read it again to be sure she had not imagined it.

At the hospital, administrators began using the new language as if it had always been theirs. "We're scaling capacity restoration," one of them said in a meeting. Jax repeated the word scaling, and the administrator nodded, smiling as if repetition were agreement. "Demand is increasing." Jax asked demand from whom, and the administrator smiled again. "From outcomes." Outcomes demanded nothing. Systems did, and systems demanded compliance while calling it participation.

Jax requested a meeting with the ethics committee. The request was acknowledged, deferred, re-routed. "This is classification, not intervention," she was told. "It sits outside our remit." Marcus confirmed it later, without surprise. "They've shifted jurisdiction. Ethics applies to treatment. This is framing."

"That's a lie," Jax said.

"Yes," Marcus replied. "But it's a useful one."

That evening Jax reviewed her original procedure notes, the language she had written when she still believed precision could hold.

Removal, not optimisation. Restraint as principle. Consent as capacity for refusal. None of that survived translation. Once capacity became the product, refusal became failure, and failure always required management.

She opened a blank document and began drafting a memo. Subject: Limits of Capacity Framing. She outlined the risks, emotional flattening, compliance without distress, erosion of refusal latency. She cited Elena, Tom, Maya, anonymized and aggregated, the kind of evidence systems claimed to respect. She stopped halfway through because she could already see the outcome. The memo would be read, acknowledged, filed. The classification would stand, and the filing would become proof that the concern had been handled.

Marcus called late. "They're pushing for formal adoption," he said. "Across carriers." Jax asked when. "Quarter end," he replied. "They want it on the books." Jax said that gave her weeks. Marcus corrected her. "It gives you days."

Jax sat at her desk long after the call ended. This was the moment she had tried to prevent, not by stopping the work, but by controlling its edges. The edges were gone. Capacity restoration was clean, legible, profitable, and once profitable it would not be relinquished. She thought of the patients together in one room, a scenario she had not yet allowed herself to stage, different histories, same absence. That was not healing. That was convergence.

Her screen lit up with a system notification. New reporting fields added. Refusal reason. Mandatory. She closed the laptop, not as protest but as recognition, the point of no return marked not by force but by classification.

The first directive arrived without ceremony. It did not announce itself as policy, it arrived as guidance, a document built to feel inevitable. Updated Reporting Alignment for Capacity Restoration

Programs. Jax read it standing, the language smooth and familiar, the kind of writing designed to make you forget alternatives existed. Participation in capacity restoration pathways should be documented consistently to ensure continuity of care and coverage alignment. Coverage alignment, the phrase placed like a bracket around the patient.

She scrolled. In cases where capacity restoration is declined, secondary review is recommended to ensure informed decision making and risk clarity. Recommended was doing less work than it appeared to, because the system would treat recommendation as expectation the moment it needed leverage.

A new field had been added to the reporting interface. Refusal Reason. Drop-down options only. Medical contraindication. Procedural risk. Temporary deferral. Other. There was no option for preference, and the absence was deliberate. Jax opened Elena's file. The field was present, empty. Elena had not refused anything. Tom's file was the same. Maya's too. The absence of refusal had become a data point, which meant refusal itself would become a flag.

Jax called Marcus. "They've operationalized it."

"Yes," he replied. "As expected."

"You said you could slow this."

"I did," Marcus said. "This is the slow version."

"That's not a defence," Jax said. "That's acquiescence."

Marcus paused. "It's containment. There's a difference."

Jax told him to explain it. Marcus did, calmly, as if explaining a protocol. "If they'd framed it as mandatory, regulators would react. If they frame it as alignment, no one blinks." Jax asked about patients. Marcus answered without softness. "They comply. Because they already are."

Jax closed her eyes. She had underestimated how quickly compliance could be mistaken for consent, and how willingly institutions would exploit the confusion. At the next administrative meeting, the language had fully shifted. "We need to expand capacity throughput," one executive said. Throughput, Jax repeated, hearing the conversion in the word. The executive nodded. "Demand is rising." Jax said they meant referrals. The executive smiled politely. "Outcomes."

Another added, "We're seeing excellent utilisation rates." Jax did not ask utilisation of what because the answer sat in every template, in every form. Utilisation of people, translated into units the system could bill, assess, approve.

Jax requested clarification on refusal handling. If a patient declines, what happens? The risk officer answered that they document it and ensure the patient understands implications. Jax asked implications for whom, and he replied for coverage, for employability, for continuity, his tone neutral, as if this were safety rather than threat. Jax called it coercion. He called it reality. No one challenged him, and the absence of challenge was the policy.

After the meeting Marcus walked with her down the corridor. "This is where it hardens," he said. "Language becomes infrastructure." Jax said he was speaking like he accepted it. Marcus replied that he accepted it exists, not that it is right, and the distinction was technically true and morally thin. Jax told him he was helping it exist. Marcus stopped and said he was limiting how it exists.

They stood facing each other. Jax reminded him he said he was a shield. Marcus replied that he was, and that shields don't stop arrows, they redirect them. Jax asked where they land, and Marcus did not answer.

The next patient declined treatment, not Elena, not Tom, not Maya, a new referral, younger, less resourced, less certain. The refusal was tentative and conditional, the patient wanting more time, and the system responded immediately. A secondary review was triggered. Documentation requested. Coverage flagged for reassessment pending outcome. The patient called Jax directly. "They said it's voluntary," the patient said, "but they also said my coverage might change."

Jax felt something tighten in her chest, a brief physical reminder that she was not as neutral as the system required her to be. "That should not have been said," she replied.

"But it was," the patient said.

Jax documented the interaction carefully. Refusal Reason: Temporary deferral. The field accepted it, and the acceptance felt like a trap. The next morning a query arrived. Clarify deferral duration. Clarify patient understanding of implications. Clarify clinician recommendation. Jax stared at the screen and understood the conversion fully now. Refusal had become deviation. Deviation required justification. Justification required pressure, and pressure would be framed as care.

She called Marcus again. "This is the line. They've crossed it."

"Yes," Marcus replied. "And now it's visible."

Jax asked visible to whom. Marcus said to him, and soon to others. Jax said that was not enough. Marcus said it has to be, because if she acted now they would frame her as unstable. Jax said she did not care. Marcus told her she should, because then she would lose the ability to intervene at all.

Jax ended the call without agreeing. At home that night she reviewed her original research notes, the early cases, the failures, the moments where she had stopped herself from going further. She had believed restraint could be preserved through intent. Intent had no standing once classification changed, and evidence could be acknowledged without being acted on.

The next day a memo circulated. Formal Adoption of Capacity Restoration Classification. Effective immediately. No announcement. No signatures. Just a timestamp. Marcus forwarded it with a single line. This is the lock. Jax did not reply. She walked to the window and watched the city move, people going to work, systems holding, coverage flowing. Capacity was being restored everywhere. Consent had become administrative.

That afternoon she received a calendar invite. Quarterly Outcomes Review. Mandatory attendance. Marcus was listed as presenter, which told her exactly what would happen. He would translate her work into acceptable language. He would protect her by making it legible. He would trade precision for survival, and that would be presented as stewardship.

She sat back down and opened a new document. Private notes, not for submission. The patterns were undeniable now. Compliance without distress. Refusal latency rising. Preference flattening. Consent becoming procedural, and procedural becoming normal. She typed a single sentence and underlined it.

Function has returned. Free-will has not.

The sentence was no longer an observation. It was an indictment, and indictments did not matter unless they could be priced. When Marcus called that evening, his voice was steady. "They're satisfied. For now."

"And you?" Jax asked.

"I'm still useful," he replied.

"That means you're compromised," she said.

"Yes," Marcus replied. "But so are you."

Jax did not argue. They were inside it now. Reclassification was complete, and the system no longer needed her intent, only her output.

Chapter Nine

The Compliance Curve

J ax stopped looking at individual cases, which was the first change she noticed, even though she still opened the files, read the notes, and reviewed imaging and post procedure assessments with the same discipline, only now she no longer treated them as discrete stories but as samples moving inside a larger system that could finally be seen when viewed in aggregate.

The dashboard helped, something she had resisted at first because aggregation felt like surrender, a concession to the very framing she opposed, yet the patterns did not appear in isolation and only emerged when everything was allowed to accumulate, so she filtered by time since procedure, two weeks, one month, three months, and the outcome curves remained clean, showing symptom reduction, functional stability, and no relapse indicators, which led her to filter by demographic, by age, occupation, and prior severity, where the curves barely shifted, and then by context, legal involvement, operational deployment, and corporate employment, until the same flattening emerged across every view.

It was not emotional absence, because that would have been obvious, it was preference erosion, so she adjusted the metrics and, instead of distress markers, tracked refusal latency, measuring how long it took for a patient to say no when prompted, which showed the numbers lengthening steadily, not dramatically but incrementally, in a way that felt both subtle and relentless.

She pulled Elena's file, where Elena had refused nothing in four months, no tasks, no meetings, no travel, no requests, and her performance metrics were exemplary, then she pulled Tom's, where he had not declined a single deployment request since clearance, had not requested rest, and had not questioned orders, and Maya's file showed the same trajectory, with public appearances increasing, consent forms signed immediately, and no withdrawal requests, which the system interpreted as resilience even as Jax recognized it as convergence.

She added a new column to her private notes called boundary assertion frequency, and the column remained empty, so she brought the question into clinical reviews, carefully and indirectly, asking Elena when she had last changed her mind, to which Elena frowned and asked why she would, asking Tom when he had last disappointed someone, which left him confused because he said it was not relevant, and asking Maya when she had last withdrawn consent, which made her hesitate before saying she did not see the benefit, all of them offering answers that were calm, rational, and wrong.

Jax stopped documenting the answers in the official system and kept them separately, while she began seeing the same phrasing appear across patients who had never met, phrases like it makes sense, there is no reason not to, and it works, as the language of efficiency replaced the language of desire.

When she requested a cohort review meeting it was approved faster than expected and the room filled with administrators, analysts, and program managers, with no insurers present even though their influence was everywhere, which left Jax presenting without slides as she spoke plainly.

"We are seeing a consistent reduction in refusal behavior, not just distress," she said, and when the analyst responded that this correlated with recovery Jax replied that it correlated with compliance, which the program manager called a value judgement until she corrected him and said it was an operational distinction, then she described Elena without naming her, a patient who accepted expanding workload without resistance, then Tom, a patient redeployed repeatedly without hesitation, and Maya, a patient whose testimony efficiency was being monetized, and when the analyst called these successes Jax replied that they were utilizations, shifting the room as the program manager insisted they did not measure preference but outcomes, which Jax said was the flaw because preference was subjective just like consent until it disappeared.

The meeting ended without resolution, which was becoming a pattern too, and afterward Marcus found her in the corridor and told her she was pushing too directly while she said they were not listening and he said they were simply reframing, turning it into acceptable variance before lowering his voice to explain they were starting to describe this as behavioral optimisation, something Jax insisted they would not do until Marcus said they already were, just not in documents she could see.

That night Jax reviewed historical cases, patients she had refused to operate on, patients who had wanted deeper relief, and patients she had deemed too vulnerable to flattening, all of whom still struggled, still refused things, still left rooms, and still pushed back, which made them inefficient but intact, sharpening the contrast as she opened a blank document and listed observed constants like refusal latency increasing over time, boundary recognition present but delayed, discomfort noted but not acted upon, external pressure interpreted as requirement, and consent framed as procedural completion, until she realized this was no longer correlation but mechanism.

She began tracking one more metric, cross patient language convergence, and saw the same phrases appear in different mouths, not taught or coached but emergent, which frightened her more than any directive because it meant the change was internalizing.

When she requested access to raw insurer feedback it was denied and she asked Marcus to intervene, only to be told he could get summaries but not raw data, and when the summary arrived two days later it listed positive indicators across cohorts, reduced volatility, improved participation, and stability under load, with one line catching her attention, reduced variance in decision making, which she stared at because reduced variance was the goal and variance was choice.

She called Elena and told her to cancel something, anything, a meeting or a commitment, and when Elena asked why Jax said because she was asking, which led Elena to say it would create inconvenience, a fact Jax agreed with, until Elena called it unnecessary and Jax closed her eyes and asked please, prompting Elena to offer rescheduling instead, which Jax said was not refusal even though Elena insisted it achieved the same outcome, ending the call shortly after and leaving Jax alone in her office doing nothing as the urge to intervene rose and fell, a pattern that confirmed the system was changing her as well as the patients.

Jax stopped asking permission, which was the second change, and although she continued attending meetings and presenting data she no longer waited for approval to look where she wanted, creating a shadow dataset that was not illegal or hidden but a parallel view built from what she already had, reorganized around questions no one else was asking, so instead of measuring improvement she measured convergence and instead of stability she measured sameness, with the curves tightening as she tracked decision trees that once diverged quickly before the procedure but collapsed afterward so that most paths led to acceptance, especially when she overlaid time and saw divergence fade not immediately but cumulatively.

The patients were not distressed or impaired, they were useful, which made her request permission to convene a multi patient session that was approved without comment because group integration was already being discussed as efficiency, so she framed it as support in a large neutral room with chairs in a loose circle and no cameras or observers, where Elena arrived first on time and composed, Tom arrived next alert and still, and Maya arrived last calm and focused, all of them nodding politely without curiosity, which Jax noticed immediately because strangers normally shared glances, tested boundaries, and assessed threat.

Jax began with introductions, asking them to say their name and one thing they chose today, which Elena answered by saying she chose to be here, Tom said he chose to attend, and Maya said she chose to participate, the phrasing identical and noted by Jax before she asked them to imagine a future version of themselves one year from now, to which Elena said functional, stable, reliable, Tom said operational, ready, useful, and Maya said credible, effective, after which Jax waited and asked if there was anything else they wanted, only to receive a stretched pause followed by Elena saying she did not need more, Tom saying this was sufficient, and Maya saying it works, with no disagreement or friction.

Jax asked what they would say if someone asked them to stop doing what they were doing, and Elena asked why, Tom said that would require justification, and Maya asked what the benefit would be, with no one saying no, making Jax feel the certainty settle so she ended the session early and, after they left, sat alone in the room knowing this was no longer inference but proof.

Later that afternoon Marcus reviewed her findings and said she was describing reduced variance, to which she replied that she was describing erased preference, while he said preference was noise that systems could not scale on and she said people did, as he sighed and accused her of assigning moral weight to optimisation while she insisted she was assigning clinical weight to consent that had been given once under conditions that no longer existed, so when Marcus leaned back and said she was asking him to argue against success she countered by saying she was asking him to see harm that did not look like harm, and when he said they would claim refusal was still possible she replied that it was unthinkable, a line he called philosophy and she called neurology, hanging between them as he warned her she would be isolated and she said she already was before leaving without waiting.

That night she reviewed early imaging again, not for lesion placement but for adjacency, and began to see something she had missed, that the excision did not just dampen threat amplification but weakened the feedback loop that flagged pressure as signal, leaving patients who still noticed discomfort but no longer acted on it, so she opened a new document for a private hypothesis that trauma circuits also encoded refusal urgency and that dampening one attenuated the other, a sentence she stared at because it described the fatal flaw she had promised herself she would never create, a treatment that worked too well.

The next morning an automated alert appeared, variance detected, because one patient had refused a follow up and the system flagged it immediately, triggering a secondary review that led Jax to open the file and see a young patient in early intervention with a recent procedure, giving her a flicker of hope as she called the patient directly and was told the refusal was because they did not feel like it, so when Jax asked what happened next the patient said they were asked to explain and then asked again until they scheduled it because it seemed easier, killing the flicker and prompting Jax to close the file and write one final note in her private log, function has returned, free-will has not, a line she did not underline because it no longer needed it, as it was no longer a warning but a description.

Chapter Ten

Controlled Exposure

The relationship did not begin with attraction, which was important, and Jax only noticed it in hindsight after the language had already shifted and proximity had become routine, because there was no moment she could isolate where interest crossed into intimacy, no rupture and no decision.

It began with alignment. Marcus understood her work, not in the way administrators claimed to or insurers pretended to, but structurally, because he understood where it could bend and where it would break, which compromises were cosmetic and which were fatal, and that understanding created relief, relief created trust, and trust created access.

They began meeting more frequently, always for work and always with a stated purpose, whether it was a briefing, a debrief, or a translation exercise between clinical intent and institutional tolerance, but the meetings lengthened and stopped ending when the agenda did, until Marcus's office became familiar, the chair across from his desk, the way he organized files, and the habit of reading before speaking all forming a pattern Jax noticed because of the absence of interruption.

He did not fill silence, he did not rush her conclusions, and he waited, which felt like respect, so she began speaking more freely than she did in formal settings, less guarded and more speculative, asking once whether refusal was not disappearing but being reclassified as inefficiency, a thought Marcus met without correction or minimization when he said that was exactly what was happening, and that mattered.

The conversations shifted gradually from defence to philosophy, not in abstract terms but in applied logic, as Jax asked what she owed a system that rewarded harm and Marcus asked what she owed the people inside it, until she asked what if the system could not be changed and he replied that then you decide how much of yourself you spend resisting it, a sentence she thought about long after she left.

They began texting between meetings, short messages, clarifications, links to documents, and notes on phrasing, the tone neutral and professional until it was not, and one evening after a particularly long day Marcus sent a message without context saying she had been right, which she read twice before asking about what, only for him to reply about where this leads, a rare acknowledgement that created warmth, and warmth was dangerous.

They met later that week at a café near the hospital, neutral, public, and appropriate, where the conversation stayed professional for twenty minutes before Marcus asked when she had started doubting herself, a question Jax rejected until he held her gaze and said she did, just without calling it doubt, which led her to admit it was when the system started agreeing with her that she knew something was wrong.

Marcus called it a dangerous insight, and when Jax asked if that was why he stayed because he saw it too, he said he stayed because if he did not someone worse would replace him, a justification she rejected until he reframed it as a containment strategy, and they sat in silence while the coffee cooled, a silence that was not strategic but shared.

They began seeing each other outside scheduled contexts, not as dates but as conversations while walking between buildings, standing outside meetings, and sharing observations neither could safely say elsewhere, and Marcus began asking questions that were not about the work, like how she rested, to which she replied she did not, something he accepted without probing, because he allowed absence and that restraint felt intimate.

One night after a late meeting they walked together without direction as the city thinned and offices emptied, and Marcus stopped outside her building to tell her she did not have to carry this alone, a claim Jax countered by saying she did not carry it but observed it, until he said she internalized responsibility and that was carrying, and she did not argue.

That was the night they kissed, not impulsively or heatedly but precisely, a decision made without discussion, and afterward neither of them spoke about it as they continued as before with meetings, messages, and strategy, the kiss existing as an agreement not yet examined.

When they did finally speak about it, Marcus said it complicated things, which Jax agreed with, but he added it did not have to weaken them, a claim she challenged by asking whether he would start protecting her because he cared or because it was useful, a question he answered by saying both could be true, which she called the problem.

Their intimacy deepened quietly, without declarations or promises, only increased proximity, and Marcus knew when meetings were scheduled before she did, anticipated which battles she would fight and which she would avoid, and intervened preemptively while she let him, a shift that required trust and surrender even as Jax told herself it was tactical and Marcus framed it as support.

One evening lying in his apartment Jax noticed something unsettling about her body being relaxed in a way that felt unfamiliar, not safe or vulnerable but unresistant, so she catalogued the sensation clinically as an absence of tension without relief, sat up, said she was okay when Marcus asked, lay back down, and found the thought would not leave her.

The next morning she watched herself agree to something she would normally question, a delay, a reframing, a compromise Marcus suggested calmly because it bought them time, and later alone she asked herself why, realizing the answer was because it was easier, a truth that frightened her more than opposition.

At work she began deferring ethical tension rather than confronting it immediately, postponing it rather than abandoning it, and Marcus was good at postponement, often telling her this was not the hill, something she believed because intimacy had created alignment, alignment had created trust, and trust had created permission, a symmetry she did not notice until much later.

The system rewarded compliance, Marcus rewarded patience, and both asked her to wait, which was how intimacy entered the structure not as distraction but as delay, reinforced by the fact that they did not talk about the future, a rule that formed without agreement as no plans, projections, or promises that required maintenance, making the present feel contained and manageable.

They met when schedules allowed and stayed apart when they did not, neither asking for more time or framing absence as neglect, which suited Marcus and also suited the version of Jax that had begun to form, especially because when they were together conversation returned again and again to work where meaning still lived and consequence remained visible.

Marcus listened when she spoke about patients, remembered patterns rather than names, followed her reasoning without forcing resolution, and often said she was not wrong, only early, a dangerous word because it implied inevitability, yet Jax let it sit because it reduced urgency and urgency demanded action while Marcus was good at managing risk.

One night after she described the group session, the room, the absence of disagreement, and the mirrored language, Marcus called it convergence and said systems loved convergence, which Jax countered by saying people should not because adaptation was erosion, leading him to ask what she would do if she acted now, and her to say she would alter the procedure and reintroduce friction, knowing that would lead to audits, isolation, and shutdown, costing patients their access.

Marcus nodded and told her she would wait, which she reframed as observing, though he called it delay, a distinction that mattered to her as she began spending nights at his apartment more often because it was easier than going home, where fewer reminders and rituals belonged to a version of herself she no longer fully inhabited.

Marcus's apartment was spare and functional, designed for containment without anything sentimental or in need of explanation, which felt safe, yet one evening lying beside him Jax noticed her internal dialogue had softened, not silenced but deferred, something she called fatigue until Marcus said she was quieter, and she replied she was thinking, though she did not answer when he said she was always thinking.

The next morning she reviewed a case and hesitated where she normally would not as a refusal flag had been triggered, and she considered intervening directly until Marcus's voice surfaced in her head telling her to let the process work, prompting her to close the file and later admit to him that he was inside her head, a truth he acknowledged because she had put him there.

They did not fight, rarely did, because disagreement remained theoretical and abstracted, but they aligned too easily and that alignment was the problem, something Marcus noticed at a dinner with colleagues where Jax spoke less, listened more, and accepted praise without deflection when an administrator complimented her for being collaborative, leading Marcus to say she used to push harder even though she claimed she still did.

Marcus told himself it was strategic, that they were buying time, though time for what remained undefined, and one night Jax woke suddenly in the dark expecting the familiar surge that had once defined her but found only neutrality, neither fear nor calm, and she turned to Marcus sleeping without tension and wondered if she had ever allowed herself to be this unresistant before, a thought that felt like exposure rather than relief.

The next day Marcus presented updated models to a consortium subcommittee, framing variance as transitional and convergence as maturation, speaking convincingly as always, and afterward when an insurer congratulated him for stabilizing things Marcus nodded, later omitting to tell Jax that he had been asked how long it would take before refusal dropped below statistical relevance, or that he had answered.

Jax meanwhile noticed patients deferring more, asking fewer questions, and thanking her for clarity, which made her feel more like an authority than a collaborator, insulating her from challenge and from correction, until one evening she asked Marcus what he would do if she said she was going to change the procedure tomorrow, and after he said he would ask why and what it would cost, he admitted he would try to stop her if she said she did not care.

"That's love," Jax said quietly, and Marcus agreed it might be, which she named as the danger, and they lay in silence without withdrawing or resolving anything, because intimacy had not replaced ethics, it had only delayed them, and that was its function.

Chapter Eleven

Capacity

E lena did not notice when the requests stopped sounding like requests, which was the first thing that changed, because they arrived as expectations, cleanly phrased and already scheduled, with language that assumed acceptance as she moved through it without friction.

Her calendar filled weeks in advance, meetings stacked, travel booked, deadlines tightened, and she met all of them as, at work, she had become indispensable, a word that appeared in an email from her manager copied to senior leadership, Elena is critical to delivery, and critical did not feel like pressure but like confirmation.

She began arriving earlier and leaving later without marking the change, her body absorbing the hours without protest as fatigue registered only as a distant signal, easy to deprioritize, so when a colleague suggested she take time off Elena smiled and said there was no need, even as the colleague watched her carefully and warned she was not invincible, to which Elena nodded and said she knew, the words accurate but without urgency.

A month later HR scheduled a performance review with a celebratory tone, growth, leadership, potential, and the HR director told her they saw her as a stabilizer who made things workable when uncertain, then mentioned an opportunity, a stretch role with more responsibility, which Elena accepted with a yes that carried no hesitation, even when the director paused as if expecting a question about workload or boundaries that never came.

Open, the director said, and the word followed Elena back to her desk.

Later that day a message arrived from the insurance liaison under the subject Capacity Alignment Update, congratulating her on sustained recovery and noting that her coverage profile had been updated to reflect full functional restoration, meaning certain transitional supports were no longer applicable, which Elena read once and archived without feeling loss.

At her next appointment Jax noticed the change immediately, Elena's posture straighter, her responses quicker, her affect flat but engaged, so when Jax asked how many hours she was working Elena said enough, then smiled faintly and said she was coping, even as Jax asked whether she was choosing to and Elena replied that it was required because the role needed it, before saying it made sense when asked if she wanted it, a phrasing Jax noted.

When Jax asked if she had declined anything recently Elena frowned and asked why she would, then searched her memory and said there had not been anything to decline, which ended the appointment early.

That afternoon Elena's manager asked her to mentor a junior colleague, saying she was good at absorbing complexity and people calmed down around her, so Elena accepted without hesitation, the sessions becoming weekly as the junior colleague brought stress, personal uncertainty, and career anxiety, all of which Elena listened to patiently without redirecting or setting limits.

When the colleague apologized for taking up time Elena waved it away and said it was fine, and when one evening the colleague asked if Elena could review a proposal late because it was urgent, Elena agreed without registering the word as demand.

At home that night Elena's sister called and said she sounded tired, to which Elena replied she was productive, then said she did not feel bad when pressed, and when asked if she felt anything Elena said she felt capable, a word that made her sister pause before noting that Elena used to get angry and did not anymore, a silence stretching as Elena said it was unnecessary.

At work her role expanded again, a cross functional initiative, then another, then temporary cover for a manager on leave, each addition framed as trust as her manager said she handled pressure well, praise Elena accepted without reaction as her calendar filled further.

At a leadership offsite she was asked to speak about resilience and spoke plainly about showing up, consistency, and doing what was needed, drawing nods from the audience before an executive told her she was exactly what they needed more of, to which Elena only smiled.

That night she realized she had not eaten, a thought that arrived without alarm, so she made something simple and ate standing, the absence of urgency feeling efficient.

A week later an internal audit flagged her workload not as risk but as opportunity, with high performers under sustained load identified for accelerated pathways and Elena's name near the top, something she learned only when a senior executive mentioned she was on the fast track and did not buckle, a phrase that did not register.

At her next appointment Jax asked when Elena had last left something unfinished, to which Elena said she did not because it was inefficient, and when Jax asked when she had last disappointed someone Elena paused longer before saying she did not aim to, then asked sincerely why she would choose that, prompting Jax to end the session and document privately, reuse escalating, no boundary assertion, capacity framing internalized.

That evening Marcus called and said they were citing Elena as a model case, which he described as stability under load while Jax called it exploitation, then recognition, leaving Jax silent because she could see it now, Elena not being harmed in a way that triggered alarms but being consumed without resisting.

The request arrived on a Friday afternoon from above her manager under the subject Interim Coverage Assignment, thanking Elena for sustained performance and noting her capacity profile made her suitable for a temporary secondment to stabilize a struggling division, temporary chosen without duration specified, which Elena accepted without comment or consultation.

At the kickoff meeting she was introduced as support, not replacement or oversight, and the team looked relieved as someone whispered she would help them get through this, which Elena heard and felt nothing as the workload doubled, the hours extended, and she absorbed it without recalibration, waving away apologies and saying this was what she was there for.

She began sleeping less, not from insomnia but from compression as there was too much to do, her body registering fatigue while her mind deprioritized it, with unopened mail stacking at home, messages unanswered, and a gym bag untouched, none of it urgent.

A week into the secondment HR scheduled a check-in, asking how she was finding the role and hearing it was manageable, then noting confidence she would cope, a word that replaced thrive, as the representative added that such deployment indicated trust and there might be further opportunities given her profile, implications Elena accepted without comment.

At her next appointment Jax noticed Elena's eyes were dulled, not distressed but depleted, and when asked how many hours she was sleeping Elena said enough, then admitted she did not track it, saying there was no need, and when asked if she wanted the secondment she called it appropriate, unable to understand the difference when told that was not the question.

When Jax asked what would happen if she stopped Elena said things would destabilize and that she would adapt, ending the appointment early again as Jax sat alone, realizing Elena was being redeployed as a resource and her lack of refusal read as availability.

At work the secondment extended quietly, the word temporary disappearing as Elena did not question it, and when asked if she would return to her original role she said it depended where she was needed, before telling a colleague anger would not help when asked if she ever felt it.

A month later she was asked to take on another stabilization project, two divisions and two failing teams framed as synergy, which Elena accepted, while her sister later told her she sounded hollow and Elena replied she was effective, letting the silence remain.

She began forgetting small things, not tasks or deadlines but personal details, names, preferences, which she did not dwell on, and one evening missed a meal entirely until dizziness arrived, prompting her to sit briefly before returning to work, unnoticed by a system with all metrics still green.

At the quarterly review her performance was cited as evidence that capacity restoration enabled sustainable utilisation, the phrase appearing on a slide that made Jax feel sick as Marcus later said they were impressed, seeing stability where Jax saw availability, even calling it consent until Jax asked to what and he replied to being useful, which made him look away.

Later Jax reviewed Elena's original intake notes, the hypervigilance, fear responses, and survival strategies that had been removed, replaced not by freedom but by compliance, leading her to write one line in a private document, reuse confirmed.

The next day an insurer liaison requested a summary of Elena's trajectory, positive indicators, sustained performance, high adaptability, which Jax did not send, forwarding instead to Marcus with the line this is not what I built, receiving back that if she pushed now they would call her emotional, a word that landed as accusation as Jax realized she had delayed too long.

Elena's reuse was no longer theoretical, it was operational, and Elena did not know how to stop it because she had not been taught how, and that knowledge had been removed.

Chapter Twelve

Redeployed

T om did not notice the redeployment order arrive, not at first, because it came through the same secure channel as the others with the same formatting and the same neutral language, the only difference being the turnaround time, immediate availability requested, which Tom read once and accepted.

He did not check the location twice, did not ask about rest cycles, did not question the sequencing of assignments, and the system did not expect him to, though his commanding officer noticed during briefing and said he had been on rotation for a while and was cleared to stand down if needed, to which Tom shook his head and said he was functional.

That was not the question, the officer replied, but Tom said it answered it, prompting the officer to study him carefully and ask if he did not feel stretched, receiving a flat no that landed without texture.

The redeployment zone was unstable, intelligence partial, assets thin, the kind of assignment that used to trigger escalation protocols and now triggered an assumption, so Tom moved through prep without friction, equipment checked, load adjusted, orders acknowledged, no resistance, while in transit a junior operator glanced at him and asked if he ever got tired, to which Tom considered and said it was not relevant, making the operator laugh unsure whether it was a joke.

The first operation went smoothly, too smoothly, with Tom taking point, moving decisively, and not hesitating when conditions changed, and afterward the team leader clapped him on the shoulder and called him a machine, which Tom acknowledged with a nod.

The second operation did not go as planned, unexpected contact, civilians present, conflicting signals, yet Tom assessed quickly and advanced and the team followed, and a warning came too late, not from command but from instinct, except the instinct did not fire.

The blast threw Tom sideways and he hit the ground hard, and for a moment there was noise and light and pressure, then nothing, and when he regained awareness he was already moving, assessing damage without panic as pain registered as information, securing his weapon, signaling status, while the medic reached him seconds later and told him to stay still.

Tom shook his head and said he was operational, she replied he had taken a hit, and Tom stood anyway, prompting the medic to swear and check him quickly, shrapnel, bruising, no obvious fracture, then telling him he should be evacuated, only for Tom to reply he could continue as the team leader hesitated with the mission clock running and asked if he could function.

Yes, Tom said, without doubt, and they continued.

The mission completed successfully, but back at base Tom's injuries were assessed properly, concussion, internal bruising, risk of delayed complications, and the medic was furious, telling him he should not have stayed in, while Tom said he was able, and she snapped that it was not the same thing, only for Tom to say the outcome was positive, making her stare and say he almost died, which Tom acknowledged with a nod and said but he did not.

That night, lying in his bunk, Tom waited for the delayed reaction, the replay, the surge, the recognition of proximity to death, and nothing came, so he slept.

The incident report was filed with careful language, operator sustained injury but maintained function, mission success achieved, and the insurer review followed within hours, rapid response, positive resilience indicators, no ongoing impairment identified, clearing Tom to continue with modified duties, where modified meant lighter load, not rest.

At the next briefing the commanding officer pulled him aside and said he had scared the medic, and Tom replied that was not his intention, prompting the officer to say Tom had not flinched, not when he should have, and when Tom frowned and asked what that meant the officer told him it meant he did not withdraw, that most people would, and Tom replied that withdrawal would have compromised the mission.

The officer looked at him carefully and said there were moments when compromise was survival, but Tom did not respond.

Back home weeks later, Tom's partner noticed the bruises and said he did not tell her, and Tom replied there was no need, while she touched his arm and said he could have been killed, to which Tom said yes, the absence of reaction frightening her as she accused him of not seeming to care, and Tom replied he cared about outcomes, which she said was not caring, a distinction Tom did not understand.

At his next appointment, Jax read the incident report slowly and told him he should have been evacuated, and Tom replied he was capable, prompting Jax to say that was not what capability meant, while Tom insisted it was exactly what it meant because he could act, leading Jax to say that was capacity, not judgement.

Tom tilted his head and said judgement interferes, a sentence that landed heavily.

Jax asked who told him that, and Tom considered and said no one, which was the most alarming part, then Jax asked him to describe the moment after the blast and Tom did so clinically, pressure wave, loss of orientation, reacquisition of target, and when Jax asked about fear Tom paused and said it did not occur.

When Jax asked if he missed it, Tom frowned and said it was not needed, prompting Jax to lean back and say quietly that this was not resilience but absence, and when Tom asked absence of what she said of withdrawal, of self-preservation, to which Tom shook his head and said self-preservation is inefficient.

Jax closed her eyes briefly.

After the appointment, she reviewed his clearance status, still green, still optimal, while the system read the incident as proof that capacity restoration enabled sustained operational output under extreme conditions, the near fatal event strengthening the case, which was the inversion.

Marcus called that evening and said they had flagged Tom as exemplary, and when Jax replied he nearly died Marcus said and continued, which Jax called not a success, only for Marcus to reply it was in their model.

Jax stared at the wall, the pattern complete, Elena consumed, Maya instrumentalized, Tom almost killed, all without distress, all without refusal, all rewarded, and she ended the call and opened her private notes, near fatal redeployment, no withdrawal, satisfaction reported, insurers praise resilience, the line no longer feeling like observation but like a charge sheet.

The satisfaction report arrived before Tom returned home, short, structured, automated, Post Incident Assessment, Subjective

Experience, and Tom completed it in the transport vehicle with the tablet balanced on his knee, answering no to distress during or after the incident, no to feeling impaired in his ability to act, no to feeling reluctant to continue assignment, and yes to feeling satisfied with his response, a pause needed only because he wanted to be precise, since satisfied did not mean pleased but correct, then he submitted the form and handed the tablet back without comment.

At headquarters, the incident was reviewed in a closed session with video footage, timeline, and decision points, and analysts focused on speed, response latency, adjustment under pressure, continuity of action, highlighting Tom's performance in green as one called it textbook and another said better than textbook because there was no hesitation, while the medic spoke once to say he should not have stayed in, quieting the room briefly before an analyst replied he was functional and, when she repeated that was not the same thing, he said it was for the model.

The conclusion was unanimous, operational resilience confirmed, clearance reaffirmed, and a note added, subject demonstrates exceptional stability under extreme conditions, a word that followed him home.

His partner read the summary over his shoulder and said they were praising him, and Tom said yes, and when she said he nearly died and he repeated yes, she turned to face him and asked if he understood why that scared her, which Tom considered before saying it was managed, prompting her to say that was not what she asked.

Tom searched for the answer and said fear interferes, a sentence that came easily, and she stared and said that was not him, but Tom replied it was accurate, and when she said he used to care if something scared her Tom frowned and said that seems inefficient, a word that landed badly as she stepped back and said she did not recognize him.

Tom felt a faint delay, not distress but confusion, and said he was improved, to which she replied that was not improvement but removal, and removal of what he did not ask.

At his next appointment, Jax did not sit behind her desk, sitting across from Tom without notes and asking why he stayed in, to which Tom replied he could continue, and when she said that was not a reason he said it was sufficient, and when she asked what if he had died he said that would have been acceptable.

The words landed cleanly and Jax felt her stomach drop as she asked acceptable to whom, and Tom said to the mission, and when she asked and to you, Tom paused and the pause stretched before he said yes.

Jax leaned forward and asked why, and Tom frowned and said because the outcome matters, and when Jax asked and you, he replied he was part of the outcome, leading Jax to close her eyes briefly and say that was not consent but surrender.

Tom shook his head and said he chose, and when Jax asked when he said in the moment, but Jax said no, he acted, he did not choose, and Tom did not see the difference, so Jax asked if someone ordered him to stand down would he, and Tom said yes, and when she asked and if no one did, he said then he would continue.

Even if it killed you, Jax asked, and Tom said yes, the certainty frightening her.

After the appointment, Jax sat alone for a long time because this was no longer erosion but inversion, self-preservation reclassified as inefficiency and death as acceptable variance, and she documented everything privately, near fatal incident reframed as success, satisfaction reported, no withdrawal, self-sacrifice normalized, entering none of it into the official system.

That evening, Marcus called and said they were calling it proof, and when Jax asked proof of what he said that fear reduction increased operational reliability, and when Jax said and survival Marcus hesitated and said survival was not the metric, which Jax said was the problem.

Marcus continued that they were asking for expansion, broader eligibility, faster pathways, and Jax felt something harden as she said they were going to kill someone, and Marcus did not contradict her, saying they would claim the person chose it, and when Jax asked what he would say Marcus was quiet before finally saying that the system worked.

The words landed like betrayal and Jax said he did not believe that, and Marcus replied no, but belief did not matter anymore, so she ended the call without responding.

That night, Tom lay awake for the first time in months, not from fear but from confusion, his partner sleeping facing away as he tried to recall what it felt like to hesitate, a sensation that was inaccessible, and he did not miss it, though something about the absence felt wrong, a thought that passed because the system did not reward reflection, it rewarded continuation.

The next redeployment order arrived two days later and Tom accepted it, while at the same time Jax opened a new document and typed a title, Alteration, staring at the word until it steadied because this was the moment she could no longer delay, not because harm might occur, but because it already had, and the system had applauded.

Chapter Thirteen

———∞———

The Efficiency Argument

J ax stopped calling them outcomes three weeks before the meeting, and that was deliberate because outcome implied closure, resolution, a thing completed, a finish line, a ledger that could be balanced, a story with an ending that made sense, while what she was seeing did not end and only accumulated. The data moved in clean arcs and the people moved in straight lines, but straight lines were not recovery, they were constraint.

She noticed it late at night after the hospital's noise settled into its lower register, her office lights still on, screens still bright, the building around her hollowing out as she opened Elena's file first because it was safer to start with Elena, no explosions, no blood, no headlines, just work. Elena's chart read like a case study in progress, symptom reduction stable, function sustained, no relapse, no distress flags, compliance perfect, yet the last item under capacity alignment was new, transitional supports withdrawn, a sentence that sat there like a compliment Elena would read as confirmation without knowing what it meant.

Jax scrolled back through the timeline and saw that after the procedure Elena's requests had stopped, not requests for care but for relief, for space, for exemption, until Elena had become available and the system liked availability. She opened Tom's file next, her jaw tightening without her choosing it, Tom's data looking like Elena's in a different uniform, function sustained, distress absent, clearance maintained, with the incident report sitting in the middle of the timeline like a bruise the system had decided was proof, near fatal redeployment, subject maintained operational continuity, subject reports satisfaction, and satisfaction was the word that made her stomach drop not because it was false but because it was true.

She opened Maya's file next, the one that never produced an obvious alarm, only clean pages and calm language the legal system rewarded, Maya's post procedure notes pristine, composed, credible, stable, with her advocacy participation reclassified as functional participation, a phrase Jax stared at, participation, the system's favorite word. She clicked into the dashboard again, the one she hated and had resisted because aggregation felt like surrender, yet aggregation was where the pattern lived, so she filtered by time since procedure, two weeks, one month, three months, and the outcome curves stayed smooth before she changed the filter to refusal latency, how long it took a patient to say no when prompted, and the line did not drop but rose slowly, incrementally, persistently.

She added another private metric the official system did not recognize, boundary assertion frequency, and the field remained empty across too many cases to be coincidence, so she closed the dashboard and opened her private notes, not the official record but the separate document she had built because the institution had no space for what she was trying to measure. She wrote one sentence and then stopped, reading it again, not underlining it this time because it was no longer a line but a description of what she was watching unfold.

The meeting on thresholds was scheduled for the next morning, quarterly metrics review, mandatory attendance, an agenda that read like routine governance, calibration, refinements, adoption strategy, forward projections, with no section for harm, and Jax did not sleep much, not because she was anxious but because her mind refused closure. She arrived early to a familiar room, the same long table, the same neutral glass walls, the same screens waiting to be lit, analysts and program leads arriving with coffee and tablets, people whose professional competence was real and whose moral blindness was also real, Marcus sitting at the far end with his laptop open and posture neutral.

Jax watched him for a moment before she stood and spoke, calm that looked like confidence but was something else, preparation, and she said they needed to talk about thresholds, quieting the room not out of respect but surprise. One analyst said they had been refining them and that they were performing well, which Jax replied was the problem, explaining without slides that their current metrics rewarded absence of distress but did not measure preservation of choice, prompting the analyst to say that was intentional because choice was subjective, and Jax to reply that so was consent until it disappeared, a murmur moving through the room as eyes flicked to Marcus and away.

They said they were seeing stabilization not disappearance, and Jax told them they were seeing delayed refusal until refusal became unthinkable, something they claimed was not measurable, to which she said it was, they just were not looking for it, then she described Elena, not by name but by pattern, increased workload, no resistance, reuse framed as trust, supports withdrawn because the file was clean. She described Tom, near fatal redeployment, no withdrawal, satisfaction reported, the incident reclassified as resilience, and she described Maya, credibility monetized, emotional flatness rewarded, boundaries unasserted not because the patient was safe but because the patient could no longer feel the urgency to refuse.

They called these successes and she called them convergences as Marcus finally spoke, saying convergence was the goal and how systems reduced risk, which Jax said was by eliminating variance, Marcus replying that variance was instability and Jax that variance was humanity, Marcus meeting her gaze and saying humanity did not scale as the room went very still. Jax said they were building thresholds that rewarded surrender and Marcus said they were building thresholds that rewarded function, and when she asked what happened when function conflicted with survival he hesitated just long enough for her to see calculation before saying the system adapted, Jax replying people died and Marcus saying that was not what the data showed, because they did not count them as failure.

They told her they could not govern on hypotheticals and she said it had already happened, describing Tom's incident without embellishment until someone said it was within acceptable risk, acceptable to whom, to the mission, and the person, he consented, at clearance, but that consent was given under conditions that no longer existed because they had altered the environment. Marcus told her she was conflating clinical ethics and system design and she said there was no separation, he said there was and that separation kept it viable, for whom, for everyone including her patients, and Jax laughed once without humor, telling him he was protecting the system from discomfort not people from harm, Marcus replying he was protecting continuity while she said she was protecting consent.

They said refusal was still possible and she said punished, no one was punishing refusal, so she told them to remove the downstream consequences, silence answering until someone said that was not feasible and she told them to admit what they were doing. Marcus closed his laptop and said this was where they differed, that she wanted thresholds preserving individual resistance while he wanted thresholds preserving system stability, and if those conflicted resistance became the cost, a sentence that landed hard as Jax watched faces show not outrage or shame but relief because he had said what they needed someone to say.

The meeting ended with action items, further review, additional modelling, no immediate changes, routine closure and procedural containment, and as people filed out an administrator warned Jax to be careful how she framed this because they would interpret it as instability, not wrong but unstable. In the corridor Marcus told her she should not have pushed like that and she replied he should not have answered like that, that they had both told the truth as they walked without looking at each other, Marcus saying she was forcing a binary and Jax replying that he was, until he stopped and told her she could not dismantle a system from inside by refusing to compromise, and she said she was not refusing to compromise but refusing to amputate choice, Marcus saying choice was not the highest good and Jax asking what was, receiving no answer as he walked away.

That afternoon the emails started, polite institutional language, follow ups on threshold discussion, clarification of risk framing, requests for supporting evidence, case examples, quantified metrics, legal implications, building a file, which Jax did not answer because she understood the trap, that if she could not translate her concern into numbers she would be dismissed as emotional and if she did translate it she would be absorbed and neutralized. Marcus called and warned her she was being logged, that impulsive responses would frame her as a risk not to patients but to continuity, and she said the system could defend itself, Marcus admitting it already was while he tried to keep her inside the room, a version of protection that was the only one left.

A week later a second meeting was scheduled, this time an alignment session with a wider invite list, governance, oversight, external observers whose presence was never explained but always felt, and when Jax saw the seating arrangement she knew it was not a debate but a demonstration. Marcus presented curves of distress reduction versus functional stability, scatterplots of wide variance collapsing into tight clustering, calling it convergence not coercion, flow diagrams of clearance gates and reuse loops, formulas of expected utility under reduced affective interference, risk heatmaps with red zones shrinking, lives saved statistically and lives spent in reuse, all while Jax challenged him that convergence was not consent, that people did not behave like systems, that the environment was coercive, that refusal could not be felt, and Marcus admitted quietly that the system could not operate on that distinction.

That was what broke her, not the model or the heatmap but the acceptance, Marcus saying he chose feasibility over ethics because every system did and he was responsible for it, and the thresholds remained without needing a decision. Afterwards governance praised his framing and Jax saw he was no longer a shield but a translator, one who protected usability not meaning, and in the corridor he told her if she kept pushing they would remove her, though really they would keep her visible and contained, and when she said she would stop asking and act he warned she would be framed as unstable unless he helped, a request he did not answer.

That night Marcus sat alone staring at convergence curves that were elegant and terrifying, feeling something like disgust not at the system but at himself, closing the file without deleting it because symbols meant nothing to the system, while Jax returned to her office and opened a blank document, not notes or analysis but a procedural draft titled Alteration, staring at the word until it steadied, until it stopped feeling like impulse and became decision, because this was no longer a disagreement about data but about value, and Marcus had chosen.

Chapter Fourteen

The Consent Paradox

D aniel was flagged before Jax ever met him, not for deterioration, not for relapse, not even for instability, but for variance, which was the kind of notice that arrived without urgency and still changed the temperature of a day.

It came embedded inside a routine internal update, the sort that usually vanished into noise. Outcome profile deviates from post-procedure convergence norms, continued refusal latency observed, recommend clinical review. No alarm language, no escalation markers, just a quiet suggestion that something was not behaving as expected, because the system did not like deviation that moved in the wrong direction.

Jax read the note once, then again, slower, and opened the attached file. She frowned. It was thin, which was the second anomaly, because most long-term cases grew heavy with documentation, layered notes, secondary assessments, addenda written to justify continued access or accelerated clearance. Daniel's file did not. The procedure had been unremarkable, the recovery clean, compliance with scheduled follow-ups intact, and nothing in the data justified concern.

What unsettled reviewers was not what Daniel lacked, but what he retained. Refusal latency remained present, boundary assertion did not disappear, and he still said no.

Jax traced the timeline carefully, watching the familiar architecture appear in the intake notes, prolonged trauma, hypervigilance, threat persistence, intrusive memory loops, the same constellation she had seen dozens of times. Procedure performed within conservative parameters, no complications, no escalation. Early relief noted, sleep restored, panic reduced, the chart reading like the beginning of a clean convergence.

Then the refusals began to punctuate smoothness.

At three months Daniel declined an optional expansion consult. At six months he declined redeployment. At nine months he declined a performance acceleration pathway. Each refusal was logged, each triggered a minor review, each was justified, contextualized, and accepted, until the pattern formed and acceptance began to look like tolerance.

Daniel did not resist care, he resisted optimisation. His refusal did not end at the clinic. It followed him.

At work the change was subtle, no reprimands, no warnings, just a quiet narrowing of scope. Meetings he once attended no longer required his presence, decisions he had contributed to were finalized elsewhere, and his manager praised his reliability while redirecting responsibility in the same breath, smiling as if it were kindness.

"You're steady," she said. "We just don't want to overload you."

Daniel recognized the language immediately, care framed as limitation and protection as exclusion, and he declined what came next in the same calm way he declined everything else. He declined the offer to shift into an advisory role, declined the suggestion of reduced hours, declined the implication that refusal signaled fragility, and each decline was noted in the only way the system knew how to note a person, as a pattern.

Performance reviews remained positive. Advancement stalled anyway.

Insurance coverage adjusted next, not violently, not illegally, just with the slow precision of policy. Optional supports were reclassified, not removed but deferred, conditional, and the letter was careful, polite, neutral.

Based on current utilisation patterns, certain services may be reassessed to ensure optimal allocation of resources.

Daniel read it twice, then placed it on the table and sat with the stillness that followed. This was the cost, not punishment, not reprisal, but alignment, the word the system used when it wanted consequences without admitting intent.

Friends noticed before he mentioned it. Invitations softened, conversations redirected, and someone joked that he had become "selective." Daniel did not correct them, because he was selective, and he practiced it in small, quiet decisions that created friction the way a closed door created a boundary. He declined an overtime request that would have compromised sleep, declined a last-minute travel assignment that carried unspoken expectation, declined to justify himself, and each refusal closed a door while each closed door confirmed the choice that had already been made.

He was not unaware of what deeper excision could offer. He had been shown the projections, reduced affect, increased resilience, smoother engagement, fewer questions, but also fewer interruptions and fewer internal alarms. Daniel understood alarms. He had lived without them once, and that was how the trauma had taken root, silence mistaken for stability, so he would not return to that silence, even if the system called the choice inefficiency.

When Jax later reviewed the non-clinical annotations attached to his file, she saw how refusal accumulated not as dissent but as drag, not as a moral stance but as a resource problem, and she scheduled him, not because the chart demanded it, but because the pattern did.

Before the appointment she was called into a short meeting, no agenda circulated, two administrators and a compliance officer she recognized but did not know well, all of them speaking with the brisk reassurance of people who wanted her to feel safe while they narrowed her.

"This is not a concern," the officer said quickly. "We just want alignment."

"On what," Jax asked.

"Interpretation," the administrator replied. "Daniel's case is being discussed."

"Discussed by whom," Jax asked, already hearing the answer in the pause.

"Downstream," the officer said. "Funding partners. Oversight."

Jax felt the pressure immediately, not overt but directional, a current that pulled toward the conclusion they wanted without stating it. "He is stable," she said. "He meets criteria."

"No one is disputing that," the administrator replied. "But his outcome profile introduces noise."

"Noise is data," Jax said, and the compliance officer smiled faintly, the kind of smile that did not reach the eyes.

"Only if it scales."

Jax did not respond.

"We trust your judgement," the administrator added. "We just advise caution in how you frame his case."

"Frame it for whom," Jax asked.

"For the system," the officer said, as if that settled it.

When Daniel arrived later that morning, Jax was already unsettled. He entered her office without hesitation, did not scan the room, did not orient himself to exits or objects, did not search for cues. He walked in, paused, and waited with the steadiness of someone who knew where he stood.

"Sit," Jax said.

He did.

"Thank you for seeing me," Daniel said.

"You were asked to come," Jax replied.

"Yes," Daniel said, then added, "but I agreed," and the phrasing registered immediately, because it was not obedience and it was not defiance, it was ownership.

"Why," Jax asked.

Daniel folded his hands loosely in his lap. "Because I thought it would be useful."

"For whom," Jax asked.

"For you," he replied, and Jax studied him, the calm voice, the lack of defensiveness, the lack of eagerness.

"That's an assumption," she said.

"Yes," Daniel replied, "but a reasonable one," and she did not correct him because she felt the structure of what he was doing, refusing to be placed where the system wanted him, even in a conversation.

On paper he should have converged. He had undergone the same procedure as Elena, the same target region, the same calibrated restraint, and he should have flattened into the same clean curve the dashboards rewarded. He had not.

"How are you functioning," Jax asked.

"Well," Daniel said. "Better than before."

"Define better."

"I sleep," he replied. "I work. I don't panic when something unexpected happens."

"And distress."

"It's reduced," Daniel said. "Not absent."

"Do you want it absent," Jax asked.

Daniel considered the question, the pause not hesitation but selection. "No."

"That's unusual."

"I know."

"Why not."

"Because it tells me when something is wrong," Daniel said, and the answer was not ideological, it was practical, the kind of practicality she had been trained to respect, and the system had been trained to eliminate.

"You could be free of it."

Daniel nodded. "I was offered that."

"By whom."

"By the system."

"What did they say."

"They said deeper excision would improve outcomes," Daniel replied. "They said it would stabilize me, make me more resilient," and he let the words sit as if he wanted Jax to hear the shape of them.

"And you declined."

"Yes."

"Why."

Daniel paused again, longer this time. "Because I didn't want to stop caring whether I was being used," he said, and the sentence landed cleanly, not dramatic, not moralizing, just a line drawn with calm precision.

"Used by whom," Jax asked.

"Anyone," Daniel replied. "Including myself."

Jax leaned back, feeling the edges of the room tighten. "You understand refusal has consequences."

"Yes," Daniel said, and this time he did not stop there. "And I accept them."

"And you accept those," she repeated, testing the certainty.

"Yes," he said again, the repetition not performance, confirmation.

"Why," Jax asked.

"Because the alternative is worse," Daniel replied.

"What alternative."

"Not knowing when to refuse," Daniel said, and the words made the room feel smaller, because they described the thing her metrics did not track, the loss of internal warning as an operational success.

After the consultation Jax reviewed Daniel's employment notes, which were not part of the clinical file and had to be requested, a separation that felt deliberate. The next request came from governance, marked informational, and she was asked to attend a cross-functional review.

The room was different from the clinical meetings, larger and more distant, screens dominating the walls as faces appeared and disappeared while connections stabilized. Daniel's name appeared on the agenda, no patient identifier, just a case reference number, and the language began immediately to reshape him into a variable.

"We want to discuss tolerance," one of the analysts said.

"Tolerance of what," Jax asked.

"Variance," he replied. "Specifically, refusal persistence."

Another voice joined, smooth, careful. "We are not questioning your ethics. We are questioning sustainability."

Charts appeared, comparative curves, Daniel's line standing apart, not dramatically, just enough to be inconvenient.

"This is not failure," the analyst said. "But it is drag."

"On what," Jax asked.

"On predictability," he replied.

A program lead leaned forward. "Your intervention restores capacity," he said. "The expectation is that restored capacity will be used."

"And if it isn't," Jax asked.

"Then the intervention has limited value," he replied.

"To whom," Jax asked.

"To the system," he said without hesitation, and someone else added the next line as if they were naming a risk category.

"We need to be careful not to valorize resistance."

"Why."

"Because resistance is expensive," the analyst replied, "and contagious," and the word settled heavily, contagious, as if refusal were an infection rather than a boundary.

"We are seeing language shift," another voice said. "Other patients are asking different questions."

Jax understood immediately. Daniel was not isolated. He was instructional.

"This is not about silencing him," the program lead added quickly. "We simply need boundaries."

"On what," Jax asked again.

"On acceptable refusal," he replied, and the phrase appeared on the screen as if it were a policy setting.

Acceptable refusal.

Jax felt something tighten. "You want refusal that doesn't interfere with outcomes."

"Yes," the analyst replied, "that doesn't propagate," and the room went quiet in the way rooms went quiet when the purpose had been said plainly.

"And who decides that?" Jax asked.

The pause lasted long enough to feel coordinated.

"Models," someone said eventually.

"Thresholds," another added.

Jax left the meeting without argument because there was nothing left to say. Daniel was not a clinical problem. He was a precedent.

The consequences were already visible. His role had narrowed, opportunities bypassed him, responsibilities redistributed not punitively but efficiently, and his supervisor described him as reliable but underutilized, the same phrase the system used when it wanted to downgrade a person without admitting it. Insurance coverage adjustments followed, certain supports downgraded, optional services reclassified, nothing dramatic, nothing illegal, just friction applied until alignment occurred.

When Daniel returned for a second appointment a week later, Jax was direct.

"You're being penalized," she said. "Quietly, but consistently, and you're aware that continued refusal will escalate that."

"Yes," Daniel replied, then added, "and I'm still refusing."

"Why continue," Jax asked.

"Because I still notice pressure," he said, "and I want to keep noticing it," and when she watched him for a reaction, for a crack, he remained steady.

"You know the system interprets that as inefficiency."

"Yes," Daniel said. "And I accept the label."

"Why."

"Because efficiency without refusal is compliance," Daniel replied, and the words sat between them with the weight of a definition.

That afternoon Marcus requested to attend the next review. He arrived prepared, laptop open, expression controlled, and he framed it the way he framed everything, as if the right phrasing could make the ethics soluble.

"This is about consent and refusal," Marcus said once they were seated. "You understand the broader implications of refusal, and you're comfortable with them."

Daniel met his gaze and acknowledged it, and when Marcus leaned forward slightly and asked the question he always asked, why, Daniel answered with the calmness that made people nervous.

"Because when refusal disappears," he said, "consent becomes decorative."

Marcus stilled. "That's a strong claim."

"It's a precise one," Daniel replied, and Marcus moved through his sequence, each question designed to force an admission into the model.

"You're choosing inefficiency."

Daniel agreed.

"And you believe that's ethical."

Daniel confirmed it.

"Even if it increases system risk."

Daniel did not flinch.

"That's not scalable," Marcus said, and Daniel's reply carried the weight of someone who already knew the cost.

"I know."

"You're asking us to privilege the individual over the system," Marcus said.

"No," Daniel replied. "I'm asking you not to remove the individual to preserve the system."

Marcus exhaled slowly. "Systems already remove individuals. This reduces harm."

"By making refusal expensive," Daniel replied.

"By clarifying consequences," Marcus said.

"And when consequences eliminate choice," Daniel said, "consent becomes fiction," and Jax watched the exchange carefully, because Marcus was not wrong and Daniel was not wrong either, but only one of them accepted the cost of being wrong.

After Daniel left, Marcus turned to Jax and said the sentence that mattered.

"He's dangerous."

"Because he refuses," Jax replied.

"Because he normalizes refusal," Marcus said, and his voice tightened as he said it, not with anger, with fear.

"That's the point," Jax replied.

"He destabilizes the model."

"He exposes it."

Marcus looked at her carefully. "You're aligning with him."

"I'm listening to him," Jax said.

"That's the same thing," Marcus replied, and he meant it as a warning.

That night Jax reviewed Daniel's intake again and saw what she had missed. Daniel had not come asking to be fixed. He had come asking to remain himself, to be stabilized without being flattened, to keep the alarms that told him when something was wrong, and to keep the capacity to refuse even when refusal cost him.

Later she opened the patient comparison matrix and added Daniel manually, not as an anomaly but as a control, then overlaid his trajectory against Elena's, against Tom's, against Maya's. The divergence was unmistakable. Daniel's distress remained present, reduced but alive, and so did his resistance. Where others converged into smooth compliance, Daniel's line remained jagged and responsive, the kind of jaggedness the system called noise and she now recognized as signal. He incurred more friction, he absorbed it without complaint, and he also avoided collapse, not because he was stronger, but because he kept noticing pressure and treated it as information.

Jax realized something the models did not allow. The system did not fear harm. It feared interruption, and Daniel interrupted by refusing, by noticing, by staying inside the cost and still saying no.

She closed the matrix and opened her private document again. Beneath the last line she added another, then sat with it long enough for it to settle into decision rather than observation.

Refusal that survives consequence is the only refusal that matters.

This was not a data problem. It was a design problem, and she was part of the design.

She added a second line beneath it, not for emphasis, but because it completed the shape of what she now understood.

Consent without resistance is compliance.

Daniel had not given her certainty. He had taken it away, and in doing so he had made her choice unavoidable.

Chapter Fifteen

---∞---

What Would You Choose

J ax's proposal to bring the patients together was approved faster
than she expected. She framed it as consolidation, group
processing, a chance for patients to compare experiences and
reduce dependence on individual follow ups, and she spoke in the
language administrators preferred, efficiency, peer normalization,
reduced clinician load. No one questioned the premise.

A shared session was scheduled in a neutral space, large enough to
feel open, sparse enough to discourage intimacy. Marcus reviewed the
proposal without comment, then looked up.

"You're sure this is appropriate."

"Yes," Jax said, keeping her tone clinical.

"It's optional," he added, as if the word itself was a constraint.

"I know. Attendance can't be assumed," she said before he could,
and Marcus studied her for a moment.

"Be careful what you prove," he said.

Jax did not respond.

The invitations were sent with careful phrasing, participation
encouraged, opportunity to reflect, attendance welcomed, no explicit
consequences for refusal. The pressure was implied, not stated, and
before the invitations went out Jax was asked to review the wording,

not formally, casually. An administrator forwarded the draft with a short note, just checking tone, let me know if this works clinically.

Jax read it slowly. Participation encouraged. Opportunity to reflect. Group normalization. Efficient use of resources. Nothing coercive, nothing explicit. She noticed what was missing, no sentence stating that non-attendance carried no consequence, no language protecting refusal, only neutral phrasing that let expectation fill the gap.

"This is fine," she wrote back.

It was. That was the problem.

The system did not require force. It required momentum, and she understood now how easily consent could be shaped by omission, how absence did more work than pressure ever could.

On the day of the session, Jax arrived early. The room had been prepared with intention, chairs arranged in a loose circle, equal spacing, no hierarchy, no focal point. Light filtered in from high windows that did not offer a view, the kind of architectural choice that felt benign until you noticed it was always the same choice.

A room designed for observation, not comfort.

She stood near the doorway and waited.

Elena arrived first. She moved with purpose, posture upright, expression neutral, and smiled politely when she saw Jax.

"Thank you for organising this," Elena said.

"You didn't have to attend," Jax replied.

"I wanted to," Elena said, and chose a chair without hesitation.

Tom arrived next, taller than Elena, still carrying himself like someone accustomed to instruction. He nodded to Jax, then to Elena, and sat across from her with the same economical movement Jax had begun to recognize.

Maya followed, quieter, composed, movements careful but unafraid. She smiled once and took a seat. Others arrived after them, two women and one-man, different histories, different reasons for referral, all post treatment, all stable. Jax knew the histories even if the others did not: one woman had survived a home invasion, another had lived through repeated workplace harassment framed as mentorship, the man had lost a colleague in an industrial accident and carried the guilt of survival.

Different origins. Different scars. The same posture.

They sat upright, hands folded, movements economical. No one claimed space, no one avoided it either. They were present without tension, and Jax registered the sameness with clinical unease because trauma usually left residue even after relief, especially after relief. Here, there was nothing left to snag on.

The room felt polished.

Daniel arrived last. He paused at the doorway, not uncertain, just observant. He scanned the room once, then met Jax's eyes.

"Is this still optional," he asked.

"Yes," Jax said.

He nodded and entered, choosing a seat that was neither central nor peripheral, not aligned with anyone, not isolated. When everyone was seated, Jax closed the door and remained standing.

"This is not therapy," she said. "There's no expectation that you share anything you don't want to."

Several people nodded, calm and immediate.

"This is an opportunity to hear how others have experienced the same intervention," she continued. "Sometimes that context matters."

More nods. She took her seat, then waited.

For a moment, no one spoke. In therapy, silence invited emergence. Here, it invited completion, as if the group were waiting to be prompted, not because they were anxious, not because they were resisting, but because that was how sessions proceeded. Elena filled the gap with the same smooth competence she brought to everything.

"I can start," she said.

She spoke calmly, described returning to work, feeling safe again, sleeping through the night, no longer bracing for threat that never arrived. "It feels like I got my life back," she said, and the sentence landed in the room like a conclusion.

Tom followed. He spoke about clarity, focus, the absence of noise, framing his experience in operational terms. "I'm functional again," he said. "I don't hesitate."

Maya spoke next. She described relief, strength, being able to speak without shaking. Her testimony was effective, efficient, the kind of narrative that sounded credible because it did not ask to be believed. "I don't feel small anymore," she said.

Each story differed in detail. Each carried the same tone.

Jax let the silence stretch longer than was comfortable. The patients did not fill it. They waited, not impatiently, not nervously, simply still, as if stillness were a skill.

She tested the pattern with a neutral prompt. "How do you handle conflict now."

Elena answered without delay. "I don't escalate."

Tom nodded. "I focus on task."

Maya said, "I let things pass."

"And when someone crosses a boundary," Jax asked, shifting the phrasing and watching for friction.

The answers came quickly. "I redirect." "I adapt." "I don't internalize it."

No one said confront. No one said refuse.

Jax felt a chill and reframed again, widening the question. "What about unfairness. Pressure that benefits others at your expense."

Elena shrugged. "That happens."

"And?" Jax prompted, holding the space open.

"And I manage it," Elena said.

Manage, not resist.

Jax glanced at Daniel. He said nothing, but he was not absent either. He was listening with the quiet attention of someone who still noticed pressure as pressure.

Jax moved through other questions that should have produced variation, how long until sleep returned, when anxiety subsided, what surprised them most. The answers were consistent, different words describing the same shape.

"I didn't realise how much energy I was wasting," Elena said.

"I didn't know how loud it had been," Tom said.

"I thought this was what healing felt like," Maya said, and for a moment Jax heard the line beneath it, the assumption that quietness was proof.

When it was Daniel's turn, he did not rush. "My experience is different," he said.

No one reacted.

"I'm better," he continued, "but I didn't want to be quieter than necessary."

Elena smiled politely. "Quiet is good."

Daniel nodded once. "Sometimes."

Jax watched the exchange, then leaned forward slightly, shifting the room with her posture.

"I want to ask a different question," she said. "Answer it honestly. There's no right response."

She paused, then delivered it cleanly. "If you could choose your future self, what would you keep, and what would you change."

The room shifted, not dramatically, but enough for Jax to feel it.

Elena answered first. "I'd keep the calm. I'd never go back."

Tom followed. "I'd keep the clarity. The ability to act."

Maya said, "I'd keep feeling steady."

Others echoed the same themes, stability, predictability, absence of fear, and Jax listened for what was missing. No one mentioned desire. No one mentioned refusal. No one mentioned anger, longing, hunger, the messy signals that made a person hard to steer.

Daniel waited until the end. "I would keep the discomfort," he said, and the room went quiet in a new way, not hostile, simply attentive.

Jax held his gaze. "Because."

"Because it tells me when something matters," Daniel said, and Elena frowned slightly, as if the answer were an error.

"Why would you want that back," Elena asked.

"I didn't lose it," Daniel replied. "I chose not to," and the line drew a boundary without raising his voice.

Tom leaned forward. "That means you're less protected."

Daniel acknowledged the statement with a small nod. Maya watched him carefully. "And you're okay with that."

"I am," Daniel said, and did not add more.

Elena pushed. "But why."

Daniel did not argue with her. "Because when I stop noticing pressure, I stop knowing when I'm being shaped."

The others listened. They did not object. They did not agree either. They simply absorbed the statement, and the lack of reaction was its own kind of data.

Jax felt a tightening in her chest and pressed the group, not aggressively, methodically. "What if refusing costs you."

Several people answered at once, overlapping in calm certainty. "That's life," Tom said. "You adjust," Elena said.

Daniel stayed quiet.

"And if the cost increases," Jax asked.

"Then you weigh it," Maya replied.

"And if refusal becomes too expensive."

Silence, then Elena answered as if she were stating a simple rule. "Then you wouldn't refuse."

"Would you notice that change," Jax asked.

Elena considered, then shook her head slightly. "I don't think it would matter."

The sentence landed hard.

Jax shifted tactics, narrowing to a concrete threshold. "What would it take for you to say no to something you were asked to do."

The answers came easily. Risk. Physical harm. Illegal orders. No one mentioned emotional harm. No one mentioned coercion, and Jax could feel the model in the room, how it sorted harm into categories it could measure and dismissed the rest as noise.

"What if the harm isn't visible," she asked. "What if it accumulates."

Maya tilted her head. "Then it's not harm. It's stress."

"And if the stress reshapes you."

"So does experience," Tom said, calm and final.

Jax felt the room closing ranks, not defensively, automatically, and she turned to Daniel because she needed a different language in the space.

"What would you call that," she asked.

He waited, then answered with care. "Erosion."

The word sat differently. Elena frowned. "That sounds dramatic."

"It's quiet," Daniel said. "That's why it works."

No one argued. No one agreed. The absence of conflict was the point.

Jax pressed one more time, naming the mechanism. "What if the request is framed as opportunity. As trust."

Several people nodded as if she had offered a reasonable premise, and Tom said, "That's different."

"Then I'd accept it," Elena said, and Jax did not let the sentence pass without testing its edge.

"Even if it harms you."

"If it mattered," Elena replied, calm as a ledger.

Jax looked around the circle. Faces calm. Voices steady. No resistance. Daniel spoke quietly, not pleading, not performing.

"I would still refuse," he said.

No one challenged him. No one followed him either. The difference did not produce conflict. It produced absorption, a smoothness that should have looked like peace and instead looked like compliance.

Marcus watched from the edge of the room. He said little, took notes, observed dynamics, and did not intervene because he had learned when not to. The session was producing exactly what the models predicted, stable affect, cooperative dialogue, no escalation, no dissent strong enough to disrupt flow. This was what recovery looked like at scale, and he noted Daniel as an outlier without elevating it into threat because one data point did not undo a curve.

What mattered was the majority. What mattered was smoothness.

Marcus understood Jax's discomfort. He simply did not share it. Discomfort was not failure. Instability was. This was working. People were stable, cooperative, safe, and the system would call this success.

When the session ended, the patients stood and left without hesitation. No lingering. No unresolved emotion. Daniel paused at the door and looked back at Jax, as if he wanted to mark the moment for her.

"This matters," he said.

"I know," Jax replied.

After the room emptied, Jax stayed seated. The silence felt manufactured, not peaceful, engineered, and she realized then what had been removed, not trauma, but resistance, the capacity to feel pressure as pressure. The room had shown her what the data could not because the data did not know how to measure absence.

The treatment worked. Too well.

Jax stayed behind long after Marcus left. She moved the chairs herself, one by one, resetting the circle into a line, then back again, as if changing the geometry could change what had happened inside it. She replayed the answers, not what was said but what was not, no anger, no longing, no hunger. They had not asked for more. They had not asked for less either. They had accepted what was given, and that was the signal.

She understood then that trauma had not been excised alone. So had friction.

The room had not failed. It had confirmed her fear, and she knew what she had to do next - Quietly.

The First Deviation

J ax did not announce the change she had made to the procedure. There was no meeting, no memo, no request for approval, no language drafted to soften intent or distribute responsibility, and no appeal to governance, ethics committees, or clinical review boards, because the procedure was hers. That was the justification she did not write down, and she no longer trusted written justification anyway. Language had become too easy to borrow, too easy to repurpose, too easy to turn against its author, so she allowed the change to exist only in practice, not in documentation.

The first adjustment was almost invisible. She shifted the depth threshold by a margin small enough to fall within acceptable variance, not enough to raise flags or register as deviation in early outcome reporting, yet enough to matter. She reviewed the protocol twice before implementing it, not because she doubted the decision, but because she needed to see where the protocol ended and her discretion began, since that distinction was everything. She was not violating procedure. She was inhabiting it.

She did not touch the target region, which would have been obvious and would have invited scrutiny she could not yet afford. Instead she altered duration and exposure time, the precise moment where relief tipped into flattening, the moment the brain stopped responding and started yielding, and she stopped earlier than the model would have preferred. Not in every case, and not consistently, but selectively, telling herself this was calibration, a return to principles that had been eroded slowly under the weight of success. Removal, not optimisation, had once been enough, and now it was not.

She documented nothing, not from carelessness, but because documentation would have forced her to choose language, and language would have forced alignment, which would have made the change legible to systems designed to correct deviation. For now, the alteration had to remain embodied, practiced, and felt.

The first patient after the change was a woman in her forties with a long history of interpersonal trauma and a high functional baseline before collapse. The intake suggested she would respond well to deeper excision, and the model predicted convergence within weeks, followed by rapid clearance for increased responsibility, but Jax stopped before that point. The surgery proceeded without complication, the markers responding as expected before diverging slightly, not enough for the monitors to register but enough for Jax to feel in her hands, in the resistance of tissue, and in the timing she had learned to recognize. She paused longer than usual before closing, deliberately extending the moment.

In recovery, the woman woke calmly, with no panic, agitation, or dissociation. When Jax asked how she felt, the woman said she felt lighter but not finished, explaining that she could still feel when something pressed, that it did not overwhelm her, but it remained present. Jax told her that was acceptable, and when the woman asked whether that had been the intention, Jax confirmed it, receiving a faint smile in return and the quiet admission that she had not wanted to lose it completely. That answer stayed with Jax longer than it should have.

Three days later, the follow-up note appeared, recording reduced distress, improved sleep, and restored function, with an additional line stating that boundary assertion remained present. That line was new, added by a junior clinician late in the evening after hours, likely after debating whether it belonged in the record or would be interpreted as noise and corrected downstream. Jax noticed the timestamp and chose not to comment.

The second altered case involved a man in his early thirties with occupational trauma and repeated exposure, who had requested full optimisation during intake, speaking fluently in the language of stabilization, resilience, and clearance. Jax stopped early anyway, and his recovery was slower, not pathological but noticeably so. He asked more questions, curiously rather than anxiously, expressed uncertainty about returning to work, and delayed his return by a week and then another, eventually explaining that he was not ready to pretend everything was fine, a phrase that appeared nowhere in the model. His clearance was delayed, and the system noted it.

Two altered cases did not yet form a pattern, but they also did not collapse back into convergence, which was the problem. By the end of the week, three more patients showed similar variance, beginning with small shifts such as rescheduled optional assessments, declined extensions framed as opportunity, and questions that could not be closed with reassurance or data. One woman simply said she needed to think, without apology or justification, and Jax marked the phrase mentally as it became more familiar.

The dashboards began to wobble, not dramatically and not enough to trigger alerts, but enough to roughen the curve and make the convergence line less elegant. Jax watched the data each evening, not for failure but for persistence, and the variance held.

At the end of the month, an email arrived from administration with a neutral subject line requesting clarification regarding outcome variability. It was careful and non-accusatory, framed as curiosity, and Jax replied with clinical language, individual context, and confirmation that there was no protocol deviation, all of which was true. The protocol had always allowed for variance. She was simply using that allowance deliberately now, instead of letting it be consumed by optimisation pressure.

Marcus did not contact her, and that absence unsettled her more than inquiry would have, because silence meant observation and the system always watched before it moved. The next altered patient refused redeployment, not because she could not perform, but because she did not want to, documenting the refusal calmly and without distress. Her supervisor recorded concern about commitment rather than capacity, insurance coverage was reviewed, support adjusted, and the patient noticed, telling Jax that she thought they had expected her to agree and she had not, describing the feeling as expensive but hers. That line returned to Jax later when she reviewed the dashboards again.

The system escalated quietly. A metrics review was scheduled earlier than usual, the convergence curve now showing visible roughness that could no longer be dismissed as noise. An analyst circled it and called it seasonal, while Marcus watched the screen without looking at Jax. After the meeting he followed her into the corridor and said she had changed something, to which she replied that she had restored something, even as he warned that the system would read it as instability. When he asked whether she was documenting the change, she said no, and he warned that this would look like error, to which she replied that erasing refusal did the same. He told her that if it surfaced, they would not see ethics but drift, and that drift would be contained, a reality she accepted without retreat.

That night, Jax reviewed her private document under the heading Alteration, adding the line that selective preservation of resistance was not neutral, then another acknowledging that uneven harm was still harm. She had crossed a line she had spent years defining, not into recklessness but into choice, no longer pretending that neutrality was possible. Some patients would now resist and some would not, some would pay for that resistance while others would be protected by compliance they did not feel, and the system would not tolerate that indefinitely.

She noticed the secondary effects first, not in outcomes but in posture. Patients sat differently during follow-ups, no longer leaning forward automatically or mirroring her cadence, and some interrupted casually, as if interruption were permitted again. One man corrected her phrasing when she summarized his response, something no one had done in months, and she simply nodded and asked him to clarify, which made the note take longer to write. Another patient asked whether a recommendation was optional, and when Jax said it was, the patient waited to ask what would happen if she declined, considering the answer before deciding she needed time and taking it.

None of this appeared in the dashboards, where what showed instead was drag, longer appointments, slower decisions, more requests for clarification, and patients asking for copies of their notes. A junior clinician asked whether refusal latency should still be logged as residual pathology, admitting he no longer knew, and in the staff room conversations shifted subtly, with nurses noting firm but polite refusals and clinicians unsure how to answer questions about whether recovery meant availability. Jax listened without intervening, aware that the system had taught everyone to read cooperation as health but had never taught them how to read resistance without panic.

At the end of the second month, a formal review was triggered for efficiency drift rather than protocol breach, held in a smaller room with closed doors. Marcus presented the once-smooth curve, noting increased decision latency that was not incapacity but cost, and when someone suggested it might be an artefact of case mix, he said it correlated with procedural variance, a word that hung in the room. When asked whether anyone was documenting a change, Marcus said no without looking at Jax, and she replied that this made attribution honest rather than difficult, quieting the room.

After the meeting she returned to her office and reviewed the earliest cases, those who had converged completely and no longer refused, reading their notes not for outcomes but for absence, for the missing pauses and hesitations where a person had weighed a request and decided. They were gone, and she realized she had altered the procedure not only to restore resistance but to restore uncertainty, which slowed systems, created friction, and exposed intent, explaining why the system would respond.

Later that evening she received a calendar hold titled Protocol Alignment Discussion, listing Marcus and two external names she did not recognize, scheduled three weeks out in a deliberate act of containment. She opened her private document again and added lines stating that stability achieved by removing uncertainty was not safety and that if resistance was treated as error, the system would remove it, then closed the file without undoing or expanding the change, continuing selectively, case by case, choice by choice.

For now, resistance existed again, unevenly and quietly, at a cost, and patients began to ask different questions about saying no, not wanting something, or stopping, while staff noticed subtle shifts in language as reluctance replaced readiness and delay replaced non-compliance. Variance became a concern rather than a threat, and Jax continued quietly, knowing the alerts would come because systems always waited for proof, and she was giving it to them one patient at a time.

Chapter Seventeen

Signal Noise

V ariance was not the word they used at first. They spoke instead about noise, small fluctuations, minor inefficiencies, natural dispersion following scale, language designed to reassure rather than explain, and the system did not accuse so much as it contextualized, even before Jax heard it spoken aloud. She saw it first in the reports as the dashboards refreshed nightly, checking them the same way she checked patients in recovery, not for collapse but for drift, watching curves that no longer settled where they once had, wavering instead, resisting flattening in ways that were subtle, deniable, and yet impossible to ignore.

It showed up in small places, a few percentage points here, a delayed clearance there, just enough to require interpretation, because variance was tolerated when it pointed toward improvement and became suspicious when it pointed sideways. At first the alerts were passive, flags marked informational, trend review suggested, no action required, and she ignored them because she was not obligated to respond until they escalated, and she knew escalation never came from instinct, only from corroboration.

That corroboration came from patients. One man asked to delay a capacity assessment for a second time, and the analyst reviewing his file marked the delay as unexplained, so Jax amended the note to read, patient exercising discretionary refusal. The analyst replied within the hour asking for clarification of the basis for refusal, and Jax did not respond. Another patient declined an optional cognitive load test without providing a reason, and that absence triggered review, coverage parameters adjusted pending reassessment, until the patient noticed and told Jax they said it was not punishment, just alignment, and when Jax asked how it felt, she replied that it felt like she had done something wrong without breaking a rule, a sentence that appeared nowhere in the system.

A third patient accepted redeployment but requested a limitation clause, the clause was denied, and the patient withdrew consent entirely, which was logged as regression. Jax challenged it with refusal is not deterioration, but the response came back annotated by a non-clinical reviewer stating refusal increases exposure risk, and exposure risk was not pathology, it was liability. By the third week, the language shifted and variance appeared, not as accusation but as observation, and Marcus did not raise it directly so much as reference it during meetings that were not about her, saying they were seeing uneven post-procedure behavior, not failure, just inconsistency, and Jax felt the word land because inconsistency was not a medical concern but a system one.

The analysts nodded. Inconsistency resisted modelling, increased oversight, required explanation, and the first formal variance report arrived on a Friday afternoon addressed to program governance with Jax cc'd, its neutral subject line reading Post-Intervention Behavioral Dispersion Summary. The report did not name her because it did not need to, comparing standard cases versus modified outcomes, noting emerging divergence in post-clearance decision latency, increased incidence of discretionary refusal, secondary effects on utilisation patterns, and offering no recommendation yet, so Jax closed it and returned to clinic.

The next patient refused to answer a question, not declined but refused, saying they did not want to explain that, and when Jax said that was fine, the nurse hesitated, which was what mattered, later asking whether that should be documented, and when Jax said to document the refusal only, the note went in even though the system did not like unannotated refusals because they slowed analysis. By the end of the month, variance had acquired adjectives, problematic variance, unaccounted variance, behavioral variance exceeding tolerance, a threshold that was never specified because everyone understood tolerance existed only as long as variance remained useful.

Marcus requested a private conversation in a neutral meeting room with glass walls, visibility without intimacy, telling her she was generating signal and hearing her reply that she was restoring it, even as he said that was not how it would be read. He folded his hands on the table and said they were asking whether the procedure had become unstable, and when she said it had not, that outcomes were being complicated rather than undermined, he exhaled and said she understood what happened next, that they would audit, but before that they would ask whether the variance was systemic or individual, and when she asked what he would say, he told her that depended on whether it continued, even though it already had.

The audit notice arrived the following week framed as support, a collaborative review to ensure protocol fidelity with no accusation and no threat, and Jax forwarded it to no one because she knew audits did not correct systems, they disciplined outliers. Patients felt it before she did as follow-ups became more structured, less conversational, questionnaires lengthened, and optional assessments were reclassified as recommended, a word that was not mandatory but carried weight.

When a patient asked whether refusing would affect coverage and the clinician hesitated, saying he did not know, the patient declined anyway and two days later her coverage was reviewed, no formal connection stated though the correlation was obvious, and she did not return, sending Jax a single message saying she thought she had made herself inconvenient, a word that appeared nowhere in the file.

By then staff were whispering not about Jax but about patients, describing them as harder to manage, more opinionated, less grateful, with one administrator calling it entitlement while Jax called it recovery. The audit team arrived without ceremony, three people with external credentials and neutral language, asking for files, notes, and outcome justifications, and Jax provided everything she was required to and nothing more. They did not ask about ethics, only consistency, whether her clinical judgement was being applied uniformly, and when she said no because patients were not uniform, the auditor said that introduced risk and she replied that it acknowledged reality, a distinction that earned a note in the margin.

Marcus sat in on the final session as witness, not advocate, while the lead auditor said variance was increasing and they needed to determine whether it reflected methodological drift, and when Jax said there was no drift, only restraint, the auditor replied that restraint should reduce variance unless the system was neutral. Marcus shifted, was asked whether he agreed, and said variance was not inherently negative but must be justified, which Jax recognized as the line, and when the auditor told her to justify it she said she was preserving resistance because absence of resistance was not recovery. Silence followed, the auditor closed the file, said that was not a clinical outcome, and she replied it was the one that mattered, ending the meeting without resolution, which was worse than accusation.

As the auditors left, Marcus remained, telling her they would escalate and frame it as risk exposure, and when he asked what she would say if they asked whether she altered the procedure, she said she would tell the truth, even though he warned it would cost her and might not save all the patients. Variance had done its job, the system had noticed, and systems did not tolerate uncertainty for long, even when the response was delayed deliberately because they waited until absorption failed before moving decisively.

Small constraints appeared in the interim as Jax's surgical list was redistributed under the justification of load balancing, with patients more likely to refuse quietly reassigned, her access to comparative dashboards narrowed just enough to limit cross-program visibility, and when a patient scheduled under her care was reassigned without explanation, arriving minutes before the procedure, the patient remarked that doctors not knowing was new. Another patient approved for surgery was denied post-operative flexibility, told she would recover faster if she followed protocol, and when she asked what happened if she did not, was told they would reassess, a word that was becoming the new threat.

Second-hand reports followed of refusal triggering additional review language, clinicians being asked to reinforce expectations, and phrases like commitment to recovery becoming behavioral standards, so when Jax reviewed the variance report again and saw a new appendix titled Unanticipated Behavioral Persistence Post Intervention, she understood the implication even before closing it. She began documenting differently, not the procedures but the conversations, noting when patients asked about consequences, hesitated, or chose uncertainty over efficiency, keeping those notes separate, not hidden but parallel.

What did not yet appear in the reports was how quickly those expectations became self-policing. Patients began repeating the language back to clinicians, asking whether their hesitation would be seen as resistance, whether slowing down meant they were failing recovery, whether wanting time would be interpreted as relapse. Jax heard it in their voices, not fear, not distress, but calibration, people adjusting themselves to a set of invisible thresholds they could feel but not see, shaping their answers before they were even asked. The system no longer needed to pressure them directly, it had taught them how to pressure themselves.

She saw the same shift in her colleagues. Clinicians who had once described patients in emotional terms began describing them in operational ones, engaged, aligned, compliant, slow, difficult. A resident quietly asked her whether documenting refusal might hurt outcomes reporting. A case manager asked whether too many optional declines would affect program funding. None of them were being ordered to change their behavior, they were simply being shown what behavior cost, and like the patients, they were learning to adjust. Jax realized then that variance was not just appearing in the data, it was propagating through the culture, a signal the system was already trying to contain.

Marcus contacted her one evening through unofficial channels, telling her she needed to slow down, and when she said she had not sped up, only stopped smoothing, he said that exposed the edges, which was the point, though he warned that governance was coming because her patients were harder to predict. She replied they were easier to recognize, a line that landed harder than intended, and when he said the system would impose uniformity if this continued, she replied that resistance would disappear again, and when he did not deny he would call that success, she sat in her office after the call listening to the hum of systems and thinking of Daniel, of Elena, of the woman who said refusal felt expensive but hers.

Variance was not chaos, it was cost, and the system was calculating whether it was willing to pay it. The answer would come soon, not as argument but as action, and when she returned to her private document marked Alteration and added a line stating that variance was not failure but evidence of choice under pressure, she closed the file knowing she did not know how much longer she would be allowed to continue, only that the system had seen her and was deciding how to respond.

Chapter Eighteen

———————∞———————

Exposure

T he audit did not begin with accusation, it began with
structure. Jax was notified through official channels, the
language precise, supportive, collaborative, a routine review to
ensure protocol fidelity and patient safety as the program continued to
scale, and scale was the justification for everything now. The audit team
arrived in phases, first documentation, then observation, then presence,
three people assigned, two clinicians with credentials too broad to
challenge and one governance lead whose expertise was not medicine
but exposure. They introduced themselves politely, asked for
workspace and access, and Jax provided what was required and nothing
more.

They began with files, not outcomes or testimonials or narratives
but logs, procedure duration, exposure thresholds, clearance timelines,
refusal incidence, return to utilisation curves. They did not ask
whether patients were better, they asked whether patients were
predictable. One auditor circled a cluster of cases and said those ones
took longer to stabilize, and when Jax replied they stabilized differently,
the auditor said that was not how the model read it, because the model
assumed stability meant compliance. The auditor made a note. Marcus
attended every session not as advocate but as interpreter, explaining

language, contextualizing intent, reframing concern as opportunity, saying Jax's work had always involved conservative restraint and that was why her outcomes were initially so strong, a word that mattered more than it should have.

When the governance lead asked what now, Marcus said carefully they were seeing the cost of deviation from convergence. Deviation replaced variance, deviation implied fault, and Jax noticed. The auditors observed procedures from behind glass, silent, watching monitors and Jax's hands, noting when she paused and when she stopped early, asking how she determined the endpoint. She said clinical judgement, they asked if that was standardised, she said no, and when they asked if it could be, she said no again, and Marcus shifted beside her because that answer had consequences. The patients felt it first as consent discussions grew longer, more formal, and less conversational, additional disclosures added to clarify downstream implications of refusal, not punishment but reassessment. One patient read the document twice and said it was different, asked if refusing still meant refusing, and when Jax said yes, added that it cost more now, and Jax said yes to that too. The patient nodded slowly and said she still wanted it, and that case was flagged.

During the second week the auditors requested a synthesis meeting in a closed room with no windows and no recording. They spoke plainly, saying they were concerned about protocol drift, and Jax replied there was no drift, only restraint, but restraint had to be uniform and patients were not. Marcus interjected that the concern was not intent but exposure because uneven outcomes created liability, and when Jax asked for whom, Marcus said for the system and the governance lead added and the patients. Jax said patients were already paying and that was documented even if the lead called it speculative. The auditors exchanged glances, said Jax's documentation was incomplete, that it did not align with reporting requirements, and she replied that reporting requirements did not include agency. Silence followed because this was not a debate, it was a calibration.

After the meeting Marcus followed her into the corridor and said she had not helped herself, and she replied she was not trying to. He said they were positioning it as risk amplification, framing her as destabilizing, and she said because she was. He stopped walking and told her they did not care about ethics, they cared about containment, and if this continued they would remove discretion entirely. She said then resistance would disappear, and he said the system would stabilize, and she realized he was saying it like it was acceptable while he said it was inevitable. That was the moment she saw it, Marcus was no longer translating, he was enforcing.

The audit entered its final phase without instruction but through repetition, the same questions asked again by different people, the same files requested twice under altered headings, the same meetings rescheduled with new attendees and identical agendas. Nothing was demanded outright, everything reframed as clarification, and each clarification narrowed discretion by a fraction. She was asked to justify why one patient had delayed clearance and she explained, asked to justify why another refusal had not been escalated and she explained again, then asked why refusal latency had not been coded as residual impairment. She said because it was not impairment, the auditor said that was her interpretation and that assessments could be wrong, and Jax understood this was no longer about deviation but about authority.

New interim guidelines appeared in draft form, not mandates but recommendations, language tightening subtly so that refusal once framed as discretionary was now described as potentially maladaptive and resistance once neutral was now associated with risk exposure. Marcus reviewed the draft before it circulated and said this was containment, that they were building a box around her judgement and asking her to stand inside it, and she did not respond because that was already happening. During observed procedures auditors asked questions mid-case, not interrupting but clarifying, asking what threshold she was using and whether it was documented, and when she said it did not need to be they made notes. Marcus took her aside afterward and said they were logging uncertainty, that it was not good, and she said uncertainty was the point, though he said it was not for them.

A patient arrived for follow up visibly unsettled and said they had asked if she had been influenced by Jax, the phrasing careful, not accused but suggested, and when Jax asked what she had said the patient replied that she had chosen, then added they did not like that. The next day the patient's optional services were withdrawn temporarily pending review. The audit notes began to include behavioral descriptors, assertive, independent, non-compliant with optimisation pathway, each neutral alone but together forming a profile. Jax reviewed the emerging framework late one night, not officially shared but circulated quietly, proposing a revised recovery index combining emotional regulation, functional readiness, and behavioral alignment, with alignment as the new variable. Marcus read it too and said this was how they solved it, the problem of choice.

Jax returned to her office after that meeting and found it unchanged, the same files on the same shelves, the same muted light across the desk, but the air felt thinner, as if the room itself had been recalibrated around her. She opened a patient record at random and saw the new annotations layered over the old ones, alignment flags, optimisation scores, risk markers replacing clinical language, and she realized how quickly meaning could be overwritten without erasing a single word. Nothing had been deleted, and yet something essential had already been removed, the quiet space where judgement used to live, where a person could exist without being measured. That, more than any formal suspension, told her how far the audit had already gone.

By the third week Marcus was no longer just attending meetings, he was leading them methodically, explaining risk tolerance, translating governance language into clinical consequence, answering questions before they were directed at Jax, protective and positioning himself at the same time. After one session she told him he was becoming their voice and he said he was keeping her in the room, and when she asked at what cost he did not answer. The cost became clear when a provisional recommendation circulated, followed by minor procedural adjustments that required no approval and could not be appealed. Jax's operating schedule was compressed, turnaround times shorter, recovery overlap reduced, discretionary buffers removed, none of it violating policy but all of it narrowing margin.

A nurse asked whether she should still flag hesitation during pre op checks and when Jax said yes the nurse said it slowed clearance, and Jax said yes to that too though the nurse did not look reassured. A registrar mentioned refusal language was now being reviewed by a secondary assessor, informal but for consistency, and patients began to arrive with preloaded expectations, asking whether resistance was something to work through or whether saying no would be interpreted as lack of progress. Jax answered carefully and truthfully but felt the narrowing because every explanation now required framing and every reassurance required boundary. The work was heavier now not technically but ethically.

Late one evening she reviewed the audit timeline and saw the same arc in every escalation, observation, modelling, behavioral framing, correction, and she was somewhere between framing and correction, which meant the next step was removal of discretion, not yet suspension or sanction but alignment. She realized the audit had never been about whether she was right, only whether the system could afford her being right, and she closed the file feeling no physical fatigue but the exhaustion of being translated. When the notice appeared reading temporary suspension of discretionary threshold adjustment pending protocol realignment, not a ban but a pause, she read it twice and saw how elegantly it ended the alteration without accusing her of making it.

She said she would not follow it, and Marcus closed the document slowly and said if she did not they would escalate, and if she did they would erase resistance. When he said she was asking him to choose, she replied she was only asking him to notice he already had. The audit team requested a final alignment meeting, Marcus scheduled to present and Jax to respond, the agenda listing risk, standardization, and continuity with ethics nowhere to be found. The night before Marcus called and said it would end tomorrow one way or another, and after the call Jax realized she was not afraid of suspension but of compliance because the audit had narrowed the field until only two choices remained.

Recommendations were drafted with softened language and sharpened impact, standardization of exposure thresholds, mandatory documentation of endpoint rationale, reclassification of refusal latency as residual symptomatology, the last one mattering most because refusal had become pathology. When Jax said this removed consent the governance lead said it preserved safety for everyone including her patients, and Marcus did not speak as the decision was deferred pending final sign off, which Jax knew meant containment before removal. That night she met Marcus outside the hospital and said he had not warned her, that he had accelerated it, and he said he was responsible for the system while she said she was responsible for the people inside it, and that they were now incompatible.

When he said if she kept pushing they would suspend her, she told him to do it, and he said they would keep her visible as an example, which she said she expected. He hesitated and said if he helped her he would lose everything, and she replied that if he did not he would help them lose everyone, and the sentence stayed between them unanswered. The audit concluded two days later with no findings, only recommendations, temporary oversight imposed, procedure continuation permitted pending alignment, and Jax remained authorized for now. The system had chosen pressure over removal, and Marcus reading the final report alone understood that neutrality was no longer possible because the audit had not ended the conflict, it had formalized it.

Chapter Nineteen

The Price of Silence

T he meeting was scheduled for ninety minutes, and it ran for three hours, which told Jax everything she needed to know before a single word was spoken. The room was windowless, not deliberately hostile, just efficient, a table large enough to hold documents without intimacy, chairs with identical posture, no visual hierarchy to suggest where power was meant to sit.

Marcus arrived early, not to prepare but to steady himself. He stood at the blank wall and rested his palms against the table, the surface cool and synthetic, designed to resist imprint. He had been in this room before, many times, usually as the person smoothing tension, translating between language sets, turning risk into reassurance, but today the language would not bend.

He reviewed the materials again, not the summaries but the footnotes, the parts no one read unless they already knew the conclusion. Refusal reclassified as residual impairment. Behavioral variance exceeding acceptable tolerance. Protocol discretion identified as destabilizing factor. The phrases were careful, not accusatory, but they positioned, and Marcus understood positioning better than anyone in the room because this was not about Jax, it was about precedent. The system could tolerate brilliance and even dissent, but it could not tolerate an alternative center of gravity.

He heard footsteps outside the door and knew it was Jax. He did not turn immediately. "You don't have to do this," he said, and she stopped beside him without sitting. "I already have," she replied, and he exhaled slowly. "They've decided. The meeting is a formality." "I know." "Then why force it." "Because silence becomes consent."

Marcus closed his eyes briefly. "You're asking me to stand against them." "I'm asking you to stop standing in front of them." He turned then. "This doesn't end with debate. It ends with you losing authority." "I know." "And you still won't adjust." "No." "Why." "Because I won't be the person who made resistance a defect."

The answer settled into him like weight. "You think I don't see what they're doing." "I think you see it clearly, and you've decided it's tolerable." He looked away. "Tolerable is not endorsement." "It's function. That's your word." He said nothing. "I can't protect you if you force this." "I don't want protection. I want truth." Marcus almost laughed. "This system doesn't run on truth. It runs on survivability." "And what survives." He did not answer.

The door opened and the meeting began. Jax entered last, not out of defiance but habit, because arriving last preserved leverage by forcing people to speak before she oriented to them. The audit team sat opposite with governance present, legal adjacent, observers who did not introduce themselves. The agenda was projected, clean and neutral, protocol alignment, outcome integrity, risk exposure, no mention of ethics.

Marcus opened carefully, not defensive and not aggressive, framing the situation as emergent complexity, acknowledging deviation without attributing blame, emphasizing shared objectives of safety, sustainability, and continuity, words designed to absorb disagreement without yielding ground. When he finished, the governance lead turned to Jax and said they would like her perspective.

Jax looked at the table, the printed reports, the familiar language repurposed into constraint. "My perspective is that the system has mistaken compliance for recovery." The governance lead nodded and said they had heard that concern, but the data did not support harm. "The data is not designed to," Jax replied.

An auditor said she had altered her application of the procedure. "I exercised discretion." "Inconsistently." "Deliberately." Marcus shifted. "That's the issue. Deliberate inconsistency creates exposure." "To whom." "To everyone, including you." Jax turned to him. "That's new." He did not deny it.

"We need to talk about control, not outcomes," Jax said. The legal observer cleared his throat and said control was a governance matter. "Exactly." Silence followed. "You have built a system where refusal is permitted only until it becomes inconvenient, where consent exists only when the cost of saying no is survivable." Marcus said that was not accurate. "It's precise." He said this was not personal. "It is, it's just not about feelings."

The governance lead said patients exposed to uncertainty might experience destabilization. "Patients exposed to certainty experience erasure." "That's a strong claim." "It's an observable one." Marcus leaned forward and said Jax was forcing an irreconcilable frame. "I'm naming the one you've been using."

An auditor referenced the provisional recommendation, standardised thresholds, mandatory documentation, reclassification of refusal latency, saying they believed this addressed concerns while maintaining program integrity. Jax read the document again. "You've turned refusal into pathology." "We've contextualized it." "You've medicalized dissent." Marcus said they had operationalized recovery.

Jax looked at him steadily. "At the cost of agency." He did not look away. "Yes." The word landed, not loud but final, and that was the moment, not the argument but the admission.

The governance lead moved close, saying they were not there to debate philosophy, they were there to ensure alignment. Jax stood, the movement surprising them. "I won't align with this." The room froze. Marcus half stood and sat again. "You're making this harder than it needs to be." "I'm making it honest." The legal observer said non-alignment might necessitate corrective action. "I expected that." The governance lead said they could suspend discretionary authority temporarily. "And replace it with what." "Uniform application." Jax nodded. "That removes resistance." "It removes risk." Jax turned to Marcus. "You're choosing the system." Marcus closed his eyes briefly. "I'm responsible for it." "And I'm responsible for what it does."

The meeting adjourned without resolution, not because agreement was possible, but because it was no longer required.

After the room emptied, Jax remained standing where she was, hands resting on the back of the chair she had not used. The silence that followed was not relief. It was vacuum, the kind that existed after a pressure seal broke. Papers lay undisturbed on the table, aligned in the same neat stacks they had been in when the meeting began, as if the argument itself had left no physical trace, only an institutional one.

Marcus lingered at the doorway. He did not step back inside. He did not leave. He looked at Jax as if she were already somewhere else, already on the other side of a boundary neither of them could yet name. "They'll move quickly now," he said. "I know," Jax replied. "Faster than you think." "I know that too." He nodded once, as if acknowledging a clinical prognosis.

"You could still soften this," Marcus said. "Frame it as a misunderstanding. Ask for phased alignment. They'd let you keep a version of discretion if you made it look like compliance." "That would make it compliance," Jax said. "It would make it survivable," Marcus replied. "For whom," Jax asked. He did not answer.

Outside, the corridor had already returned to its ordinary rhythm, staff moving between offices, data carts rolling past, voices low and procedural. No one looked at her. No one needed to. The decision was no longer visible. It had been internalized.

Jax walked past the audit team without acknowledgment. They were already speaking to each other in the language of follow-up, of action items, of transitional oversight. The confrontation had been absorbed and converted.

In the elevator, she watched her reflection in the metal panel. She looked unchanged. No visible mark of conflict. That was the danger. Systems that erased resistance did not leave scars. They left smoothness. Her phone vibrated once, not a message but a calendar update. Alignment Review. Two days from now. Attendance mandatory. She did not open it.

Back in her office, she closed the door and leaned against it, not from weakness but from stillness, letting the weight of the building press back. The confrontation had not been loud. It had been decisive. That was worse. They had not needed to defeat her. They had simply named her as incompatible.

For the first time since she altered the procedure, Jax felt the full shape of the risk she had introduced, not to the patients but to herself, and she did not regret it. She opened her private document, the one the system could not see, and added nothing. There was nothing left to justify. The confrontation had done what documentation never could. It had made the stakes explicit. Choice was now visible, and that was why it would be punished.

The punishment did not arrive as an order. It arrived as access changes. Her dashboard loaded more slowly. Her scheduling system inserted extra approval layers. Names that once appeared as green now showed amber, pending review. No one told her this was disciplinary. It was framed as optimisation. She knew what it meant. The system was beginning to place her inside a smaller world.

A message arrived from clinical oversight requesting clarification on three recent cases. Not accusations, clarifications, the kind that forced her to justify every deviation from the median. Each question assumed she had erred and was waiting to be corrected. She closed the window without responding.

Jax moved to the observation glass and looked down at the recovery ward below. Patients lay in soft-lit rooms, neural monitors glowing faintly, their faces calm in the way only chemically assisted equilibrium could produce. From here everything looked stable. That was the illusion the system had always sold. Stability meant success. Variance meant risk. Choice meant noise.

She thought of the woman who had refused the final compression phase and had been allowed to leave with memory intact, of the tremor in her hands when she signed the release form, the fear mixed with something else, something almost like pride. That patient would not exist in the data. She would exist only in Jax. That was the real threat.

A knock sounded at her door. Not security, not governance, one of her registrars, pale, careful, carrying a tablet like a shield. "They've locked the late clearance queue," he said quietly. "Only standard profiles can be processed now." Jax nodded. "How long." "Until further notice." The registrar hesitated. "They're saying it's temporary." "Everything is," Jax replied.

He did not ask what that meant. He thanked her and left.

Jax returned to her desk and sat, not to work but to think. The confrontation had not been designed to remove her. It had been designed to isolate her, to make her the last node of a dying pattern, so that when it disappeared no one would notice except her. That was how systems killed ideas.

Marcus's face came back to her, the moment he said yes, not loudly, not cruelly, just accurately. Agency was a cost the system had decided it could no longer afford. He had known it before she had. That was why he was dangerous, not because he was wrong, but because he was right in a way that served power.

Her phone vibrated again, this time a message from Marcus. *I meant what I said. They will not stop with you. They will use you.* Jax did not reply. Another followed. *If you go quiet now, you can still keep some leverage.* She closed the message without responding. Leverage was another word for delay, and delay was how erasure happened gently.

Instead she opened her private archive, the unindexed space she had created months ago, long before the audit, when she had realized that some data should never be optimized. Inside were transcripts, patient narratives, raw choice unfiltered by scoring models, stories of refusal, hesitation, ambivalence, human noise. She added one line at the top of the file.

If this disappears, you were here.

Not signed. Not encrypted. Just written, a warning or a memorial.

Outside, night was settling across the hospital, the city lights flickering on like a network coming online. Jax stayed where she was. The confrontation had ended, but the conflict had only just begun. Now it was quiet enough to hear the real machinery - **Chapter 19 – Confrontation**

The meeting was scheduled for ninety minutes, and it ran for three hours, which told Jax everything she needed to know before a single word was spoken. The room was windowless, not deliberately hostile, just efficient, a table large enough to hold documents without intimacy, chairs with identical posture, no visual hierarchy to suggest where power was meant to sit.

Marcus arrived early, not to prepare but to steady himself. He stood at the blank wall and rested his palms against the table, the surface cool and synthetic, designed to resist imprint. He had been in this room before, many times, usually as the person smoothing tension, translating between language sets, turning risk into reassurance, but today the language would not bend.

He reviewed the materials again, not the summaries but the footnotes, the parts no one read unless they already knew the conclusion. Refusal reclassified as residual impairment. Behavioral variance exceeding acceptable tolerance. Protocol discretion identified as destabilizing factor. The phrases were careful, not accusatory, but they positioned, and Marcus understood positioning better than anyone in the room because this was not about Jax, it was about precedent. The system could tolerate brilliance and even dissent, but it could not tolerate an alternative center of gravity.

He heard footsteps outside the door and knew it was Jax. He did not turn immediately. "You don't have to do this," he said, and she stopped beside him without sitting. "I already have," she replied, and he exhaled slowly. "They've decided. The meeting is a formality." "I know." "Then why force it." "Because silence becomes consent."

Marcus closed his eyes briefly. "You're asking me to stand against them." "I'm asking you to stop standing in front of them." He turned then. "This doesn't end with debate. It ends with you losing authority." "I know." "And you still won't adjust." "No." "Why." "Because I won't be the person who made resistance a defect."

The answer settled into him like weight. "You think I don't see what they're doing." "I think you see it clearly, and you've decided it's tolerable." He looked away. "Tolerable is not endorsement." "It's function. That's your word." He said nothing. "I can't protect you if you force this." "I don't want protection. I want truth." Marcus almost laughed. "This system doesn't run on truth. It runs on survivability." "And what survives." He did not answer.

The door opened and the meeting began. Jax entered last, not out of defiance but habit, because arriving last preserved leverage by forcing people to speak before she oriented to them. The audit team sat opposite with governance present, legal adjacent, observers who did not introduce themselves. The agenda was projected, clean and neutral, protocol alignment, outcome integrity, risk exposure, no mention of ethics.

Marcus opened carefully, not defensive and not aggressive, framing the situation as emergent complexity, acknowledging deviation without attributing blame, emphasizing shared objectives of safety, sustainability, and continuity, words designed to absorb disagreement without yielding ground. When he finished, the governance lead turned to Jax and said they would like her perspective.

Jax looked at the table, the printed reports, the familiar language repurposed into constraint. "My perspective is that the system has mistaken compliance for recovery." The governance lead nodded and said they had heard that concern, but the data did not support harm. "The data is not designed to," Jax replied.

An auditor said she had altered her application of the procedure. "I exercised discretion." "Inconsistently." "Deliberately." Marcus shifted. "That's the issue. Deliberate inconsistency creates exposure."

"To whom." "To everyone, including you." Jax turned to him. "That's new." He did not deny it.

"We need to talk about control, not outcomes," Jax said. The legal observer cleared his throat and said control was a governance matter. "Exactly." Silence followed. "You have built a system where refusal is permitted only until it becomes inconvenient, where consent exists only when the cost of saying no is survivable." Marcus said that was not accurate. "It's precise." He said this was not personal. "It is, it's just not about feelings."

The governance lead said patients exposed to uncertainty might experience destabilization. "Patients exposed to certainty experience erasure." "That's a strong claim." "It's an observable one." Marcus leaned forward and said Jax was forcing an irreconcilable frame. "I'm naming the one you've been using."

An auditor referenced the provisional recommendation, standardised thresholds, mandatory documentation, reclassification of refusal latency, saying they believed this addressed concerns while maintaining program integrity. Jax read the document again. "You've turned refusal into pathology." "We've contextualized it." "You've medicalized dissent." Marcus said they had operationalized recovery. Jax looked at him steadily. "At the cost of agency." He did not look away. "Yes." The word landed, not loud but final, and that was the moment, not the argument but the admission.

The governance lead moved close, saying they were not there to debate philosophy, they were there to ensure alignment. Jax stood, the movement surprising them. "I won't align with this." The room froze. Marcus half stood and sat again. "You're making this harder than it needs to be." "I'm making it honest." The legal observer said non-alignment might necessitate corrective action. "I expected that." The governance lead said they could suspend discretionary authority temporarily. "And replace it with what." "Uniform application." Jax nodded. "That removes resistance." "It removes risk." Jax turned to Marcus. "You're choosing the system." Marcus closed his eyes briefly. "I'm responsible for it." "And I'm responsible for what it does."

The meeting adjourned without resolution, not because agreement was possible, but because it was no longer required.

After the room emptied, Jax remained standing where she was, hands resting on the back of the chair she had not used. The silence that followed was not relief. It was vacuum, the kind that existed after a pressure seal broke. Papers lay undisturbed on the table, aligned in the same neat stacks they had been in when the meeting began, as if the argument itself had left no physical trace, only an institutional one.

Marcus lingered at the doorway. He did not step back inside. He did not leave. He looked at Jax as if she were already somewhere else, already on the other side of a boundary neither of them could yet name. "They'll move quickly now," he said. "I know," Jax replied. "Faster than you think." "I know that too." He nodded once, as if acknowledging a clinical prognosis.

"You could still soften this," Marcus said. "Frame it as a misunderstanding. Ask for phased alignment. They'd let you keep a version of discretion if you made it look like compliance." "That would make it compliance," Jax said. "It would make it survivable," Marcus replied. "For whom," Jax asked. He did not answer.

Outside, the corridor had already returned to its ordinary rhythm, staff moving between offices, data carts rolling past, voices low and procedural. No one looked at her. No one needed to. The decision was no longer visible. It had been internalized.

Jax walked past the audit team without acknowledgment. They were already speaking to each other in the language of follow-up, of action items, of transitional oversight. The confrontation had been absorbed and converted.

In the elevator, she watched her reflection in the metal panel. She looked unchanged. No visible mark of conflict. That was the danger. Systems that erased resistance did not leave scars. They left smoothness. Her phone vibrated once, not a message but a calendar update. Alignment Review. Two days from now. Attendance mandatory. She did not open it.

Back in her office, she closed the door and leaned against it, not from weakness but from stillness, letting the weight of the building press back. The confrontation had not been loud. It had been decisive. That was worse. They had not needed to defeat her. They had simply named her as incompatible.

For the first time since she altered the procedure, Jax felt the full shape of the risk she had introduced, not to the patients but to herself, and she did not regret it. She opened her private document, the one the system could not see, and added nothing. There was nothing left to justify. The confrontation had done what documentation never could. It had made the stakes explicit. Choice was now visible, and that was why it would be punished.

The punishment did not arrive as an order. It arrived as access changes. Her dashboard loaded more slowly. Her scheduling system inserted extra approval layers. Names that once appeared as green now showed amber, pending review. No one told her this was disciplinary. It was framed as optimisation. She knew what it meant. The system was beginning to place her inside a smaller world.

A message arrived from clinical oversight requesting clarification on three recent cases. Not accusations, clarifications, the kind that forced her to justify every deviation from the median. Each question assumed she had erred and was waiting to be corrected. She closed the window without responding.

Jax moved to the observation glass and looked down at the recovery ward below. Patients lay in soft-lit rooms, neural monitors glowing faintly, their faces calm in the way only chemically assisted equilibrium could produce. From here everything looked stable. That was the illusion the system had always sold. Stability meant success. Variance meant risk. Choice meant noise.

She thought of the woman who had refused the final compression phase and had been allowed to leave with memory intact, of the tremor in her hands when she signed the release form, the fear mixed with something else, something almost like pride. That patient would not exist in the data. She would exist only in Jax. That was the real threat.

A knock sounded at her door. Not security, not governance, one of her registrars, pale, careful, carrying a tablet like a shield. "They've locked the late clearance queue," he said quietly. "Only standard profiles can be processed now." Jax nodded. "How long." "Until further notice." The registrar hesitated. "They're saying it's temporary." "Everything is," Jax replied.

He did not ask what that meant. He thanked her and left.

Jax returned to her desk and sat, not to work but to think. The confrontation had not been designed to remove her. It had been designed to isolate her, to make her the last node of a dying pattern, so that when it disappeared no one would notice except her. That was how systems killed ideas.

Marcus's face came back to her, the moment he said yes, not loudly, not cruelly, just accurately. Agency was a cost the system had decided it could no longer afford. He had known it before she had. That was why he was dangerous, not because he was wrong, but because he was right in a way that served power.

Her phone vibrated again, this time a message from Marcus. *I meant what I said. They will not stop with you. They will use you.* Jax did not reply. Another followed. *If you go quiet now, you can still keep some leverage.* She closed the message without responding. Leverage was another word for delay, and delay was how erasure happened gently.

Instead she opened her private archive, the unindexed space she had created months ago, long before the audit, when she had realized that some data should never be optimized. Inside were transcripts, patient narratives, raw choice unfiltered by scoring models, stories of refusal, hesitation, ambivalence, human noise. She added one line at the top of the file.

If this disappears, you were here.

Not signed. Not encrypted. Just written, a warning or a memorial.

Outside, night was settling across the hospital, the city lights flickering on like a network coming online. Jax stayed where she was. The confrontation had ended, but the conflict had only just begun. Now it was quiet enough to hear the real machinery - and she listened.

Chapter Twenty

---∽⌣∾---

Risk Mitigation

Containment did not arrive with an announcement. It arrived with subtraction.

Jax noticed it first in her schedule, not as cancellations but as reallocations, small adjustments framed as operational efficiency, a case reassigned here, a follow up deferred there, nothing dramatic enough to challenge but enough to narrow her reach. Her operating list shortened by two procedures the first week, no explanation offered, and when she asked, the response was neutral, a sequence of phrases rather than an answer: load balancing, optimisation, coverage continuity, language that did not accuse but did not answer either.

She reviewed the reassigned cases and saw what they shared. Patients with higher refusal probability, patients flagged as decision variable, patients who had begun asking questions that slowed throughput. Containment was not punishment, it was filtration.

Her access changed next. Dashboards that had once opened automatically now required secondary authentication, certain comparative views no longer visible to her role. She requested access and the request sat, not denied but pending, a distinction that mattered because pending meant observed and pending meant leverage.

Her email traffic thinned. Messages from patients increased, messages from administration slowed, replies arriving later and with fewer words. Where she had once been consulted, she was now informed. Where she had once shaped language, she now received it, reading every sentence carefully because containment did not hide itself, it disguised itself as care.

A memo arrived midweek, subject line Interim Oversight Measures. The language was precise. To ensure program continuity during alignment review, discretionary procedural adjustments would require secondary sign off, though from whom was not specified. Jax read the memo twice and understood that this did not suspend her, it neutralized her. She continued to operate, but she no longer decided alone.

The first request for sign off arrived that afternoon, a routine borderline optimisation case, exactly the kind she had altered quietly in recent weeks. She submitted her rationale, clinical judgement, preservation of agency, risk mitigation through retained refusal, and the response came back three hours later: request denied, proceed per standard parameters. She stared at the screen longer than necessary, then closed it.

The next patient asked whether the procedure would be the same as before. Jax said yes. The patient asked which before, and the question landed harder than it should have. Jax explained carefully, the patient listened, then asked if she wanted the version where she could still say no. Jax paused and said that depended on authorization. The patient nodded slowly and said she had thought it was her brain, and Jax replied that it was, though the distinction no longer reassured either of them.

Marcus did not contact her. That absence was deliberate because containment required separation. When he did appear, it was formally, a calendar invitation marked Alignment Follow Up, mandatory. He sat across from her in another neutral room, this one smaller, and said he had tried to slow it. Jax replied that he had translated it, that it had kept her inside something he would not name. He said they had reassigned some of her cases, that they were concerned about uneven exposure, and Jax replied that they had created it.

Marcus looked tired now, not conflicted but narrowed. He said she was being managed, that she was still pushing, that it made this harder, and Jax replied that it made it honest. He said they were asking whether continued variance was intentional, that he had told them it was complex. Jax called it a lie. Marcus agreed, but said it was a useful one.

She stood. She said she would not ask him to protect her, only one thing instead, that when they came for the patients he should not call it recovery. Marcus did not answer. That was his answer.

The patients felt containment more sharply than she did. One arrived agitated. Case management had asked him to justify his refusal, just needing context, they said. He told them he did not want to. They scheduled another assessment, which concluded with a recommendation for increased support, and support meant oversight. Another patient stopped attending follow ups entirely and sent Jax a message saying she did not want to be measured anymore. The sentence had no place in the system, so Jax saved it anyway.

Staff behavior shifted. Colleagues who once consulted her now avoided eye contact, not out of hostility but caution, because association had become risk. A registrar asked whether refusal should still be encouraged during consent discussions. Jax said encouraged was the wrong word and told him to say that it existed. He nodded, unconvinced.

Later that week a notice appeared on her terminal. Procedure authorization pending review, temporary hold. She contacted administration and the response arrived quickly. Her authorization had not been revoked, additional review was required for alignment purposes. Alignment again. Containment did not need to accuse, it only needed to slow.

She continued working. She documented meticulously, not to comply but to record, noting every denied sign off, every reassigned case, every patient question that could not be closed cleanly. Her private document grew, not analysis but evidence. At night she reviewed the earliest cases again, those who had converged completely, those who had stopped refusing, and she saw them differently now, not as successes but as absences.

Containment reached its final form when a new role appeared, Program Clinical Liaison. The liaison attended her procedures, sat quietly, took notes, did not interfere. Presence was enough. When Jax asked if she was being supervised, the liaison replied that she was being supported, the difference purely cosmetic.

Marcus attended the first session with the liaison and did not meet Jax's eyes. Afterward she confronted him and said this was his solution. He said it was survival, for the program, and when she added and the patients, he looked away.

Containment worked because it did not provoke. It exhausted.

By the end of the month Jax's discretion existed only in theory. She could still speak and still recommend, but the system had learned how to wait her out. Time itself changed. Days no longer ended cleanly, meetings bled into documentation, documentation into follow ups that felt administrative rather than clinical. She was asked to justify language, not decisions.

A phrase she had used for years was flagged, preservation of agency. The reviewer suggested replacing it with functional autonomy. Jax said no because autonomy without refusal was decorative. The reviewer noted disagreement. Disagreement was becoming a category.

A second memo arrived, Clarification on Consent Framing, suggesting updated phrasing so patients would not misunderstand refusal as endorsement of suboptimal outcomes. Refusal acknowledged, discouraged. Jax returned it without comment. It came back unchanged.

The next patient asked whether choosing not to proceed would reflect poorly on her recovery profile. Jax said yes, and when the patient said that was new, Jax replied that it was just visible now. The patient laughed without humor, saying that if she complied she was well and if she did not she was complicated. Jax said yes. The patient nodded and complied, not because she wanted to but because she understood, a distinction that haunted Jax more than refusal ever had.

The liaison began asking questions after procedures, not accusatory but curious, asking why Jax had stopped when she did. Jax said because going further would flatten response, that flattening response was bad for consent. The liaison wrote something down. Jax never saw what.

Marcus messaged her one evening that they needed to talk. She did not reply. He appeared the next day and said this was not working. Jax said that was the point. He said they were losing patience and asked whether she was still aligned with program goals. When she asked what those were, he did not answer. Jax said that silence was his answer and noticed how often Marcus now avoided her eyes, not from shame but from calculation.

Containment reached patients differently. Those with institutional roles felt it as pressure. Those without felt it as disappearance. Appointment reminders stopped, insurance portals locked pending review, satisfaction surveys arrived before recovery had ended. One patient left hers blank, triggering a call asking for anything at all, and she replied that anything was not fine. She told Jax later that they wanted affirmation, not feedback, and that she thought she had liked it better when she was scared.

Containment altered her colleagues too, not their opinions but their behavior. They deferred more often, waited for permission they once would have given. Clinical confidence became procedural caution. One colleague whispered that they had been told not to ask Jax anything that could be interpreted, and interpreted was doing a lot of work.

The building itself felt different. Badge readers paused, a half second delay that was enough to remind. Jax documented it all mentally because containment was not a single action, it was a thousand small frictions designed to make resistance expensive, and it was working.

She moved differently now, speaking less, choosing words more carefully, then fewer of them. Silence became safer than explanation. She waited more often, outside offices, outside meetings, outside decisions she had once shaped. Waiting placed her after the fact.

One afternoon she realized she had not been asked for input on a case she had designed the protocol for. She was cc'd on the outcome, approved, proceed per standard parameters, her name nowhere in the trail. The patient had converged completely, no refusal, no hesitation, no delay, exemplary outcome. Jax felt the urge to intervene, not clinically but ethically, to name what had been removed, and she did not.

Containment taught restraint differently, not as care but as disappearance.

By the end of the week she understood that nothing else needed to happen for the system to succeed. It only needed her to remain, present, quiet, aligned by inertia. That was when she felt it, not fear but resolve. She knew what came next, suspension not as punishment but as precaution.

She prepared quietly, not to fight but to endure. She archived her private notes internally. She did not yet know how they would be used, only that they mattered. Containment was not the end. It was a holding pattern, and holding patterns always preceded correction.

---◇◇◇---

Chapter Twenty-one

The Cover Story

Marcus understood the system well enough to know that truth rarely failed because it was wrong, it failed because it arrived in the wrong format. He had spent years translating complexity into stability, turning ambiguity into dashboards, turning harm into tolerable variance, and he knew exactly how much distortion the system could absorb without rejecting the signal entirely. What he had never tested was whether it could be bent deliberately without breaking him first.

The opportunity arrived as a routine request. Subject, Variance Reconciliation Update. Sender, Program Governance. Deadline, end of week. The request was framed as clarification, a final alignment exercise to reconcile divergent data streams ahead of formal resolution, and Marcus was asked to consolidate findings and propose a narrative that accounted for recent instability while preserving confidence. Preserving confidence was the real task.

He read the message twice, then once more, slower. He did not forward it, did not acknowledge receipt, and let it sit, because silence was the first signal the system always sent before pressure followed. Then he opened the raw data, not the dashboards or the executive summaries, but the feeds beneath them, timestamped entries, manual annotations, edge cases that had been tagged and then ignored because they resisted categorization.

He began with the convergence curves. He knew where they had been smoothed, had authorized some of those adjustments himself months earlier when scale had still felt like progress, and knew which assumptions had been carried forward unchallenged because they produced clean lines. Refusal latency was one of them, not excluded, just diminished, down weighted, reframed as transitional noise.

Marcus isolated the variable and the model shifted immediately, not dramatically, just enough. He adjusted the weighting again and this time the curve did not tighten toward convergence, it flattened toward dispersion with stability. The system would not like that, but it might tolerate it if the explanation arrived slowly enough and sounded procedural rather than ideological.

He worked through the night, not furtively but methodically. Marcus did not rush, because rushing created error, and error was the one thing the system could not forgive. He approached the task the way he approached governance reviews, by assuming every conclusion would be challenged by someone more patient than him, someone waiting for him to overstate so they could punish the overstatement instead of the finding.

He rebuilt the assumptions one at a time. The original convergence model assumed affective dampening correlated directly with reduced risk, an assumption never proven, merely inherited from frameworks that privileged stability over agency. Marcus adjusted the baseline and introduced a decay variable, not for distress but for compliance, the longer a patient remained flattened, the more likely they were to accept risk they would previously have resisted. That variable had never been measured.

He did not invent data. He used indicators that already existed but had never been grouped, reuse frequency, escalation acceptance, post event reporting delays, the things that happened after success was declared. The pattern emerged slowly. Flattened patients did not fail more often, they failed later, and delayed failure was harder to attribute, harder to trace back to intervention, easier to absorb as ambient loss. Marcus understood then why the system preferred it.

He adjusted the model again, this time comparing early resistance against long term utilisation outcomes. The curve bent. Resistance was not inefficiency, it was a buffer, and buffers slowed systems, but they also prevented collapse.

He saved the version under a neutral filename, Variance_Reconciliation_v3, then opened the governance language template. He did not write conclusions, he wrote options. Option A framed variance as transient instability requiring correction. Option B framed variance as adaptive redistribution requiring monitoring. Option C framed variance as artefact of scale requiring delayed intervention. He highlighted Option B, not because it was safest, but because it was hardest to reject outright. The system hated absolutes, it preferred postponement dressed as prudence.

He prepared supplementary notes, not for the meeting but for the conversations after it, the corridor questions, the inbox clarifications, the unscheduled calls. He knew they would come. He did not sleep.

By morning his body felt hollow, but his mind did not. When he arrived at the meeting the room felt different, less tension, more caution. People were curious rather than confrontational, which told him his reframing had already circulated. He delivered the presentation without flourish, no emphasis, no moral language, just system logic turned slightly off axis.

When legal frowned, Marcus slowed. When governance leaned back, he continued. When an analyst nodded, he stopped. The rhythm mattered. By the end, no one was convinced, but no one was ready to override him either, and that was success.

Marcus learned quickly that hesitation produced questions, not formal ones, not yet. They arrived sideways, a calendar invitation without agenda, a forwarded thread missing its origin, a request for clarification that arrived already pre interpreted. The system did not accuse, it triangulated.

On the second day after the meeting, governance asked for a sensitivity analysis, not urgent, just helpful, a way to stress test assumptions before escalation. Marcus complied, producing three versions of the same model, each weighted differently, each technically defensible, and he did not indicate preference. He let the numbers sit beside each other and waited to see which one the room leaned toward. No one leaned, and that unsettled him more than disagreement would have.

On the third day, legal asked whether his reframing introduced exposure under existing coverage language, framed as curiosity, a hypothetical. Marcus responded with precedent, older programs, sunset clauses, tolerated ambiguity during early scaling phases. Legal acknowledged the response but did not close the question.

By the fourth day, Marcus noticed the pattern. No single request was aggressive, no message carried threat, but the volume increased, each interaction shaving a margin, each clarification demanding another hour, another justification, another recalculation. The system was not pushing back, it was slowing him down.

He adjusted his behavior, and stopped responding immediately, letting delay create room, scheduling replies for early morning or late evening, times that implied diligence rather than defensiveness, framing follow ups as continuity, not resistance. Still, the pressure mounted.

A governance analyst asked to sit in on one of his modelling sessions, not to audit but to understand. Marcus agreed. She watched quietly as he manipulated variables, asking questions that appeared naive but were not, about refusal stabilizing without resolving, compliance declining after an initial gain, and institutional patience. Marcus answered all of them, knowing none of them were neutral.

After she left, he realized he had crossed a line he could not uncross. He had made refusal visible, not ethically but mechanically, and the system could tolerate ethics as commentary, but it struggled with mechanics that disrupted predictability.

That night Marcus slept poorly, not because he was afraid but because he was calculating. He ran scenarios, best case, worst case, most likely, mapping outcomes across timelines. In the best case, his reframing bought sustained delay and Jax retained space. In the worst, governance reclassified his modelling as error and revoked his access. In the most likely, the system absorbed his work, stripped it of intent, and kept moving.

Marcus understood then that he was not indispensable, he never had been. The system had tolerated him because he translated well, and if he stopped translating in the direction it preferred, it would simply find someone else.

On the fifth day the questions changed tone. A governance lead asked whether the current instability reflected a temporary adjustment phase or a structural flaw. Temporary meant patience. Structural meant intervention. Marcus replied that it was too early to distinguish, and that answer bought him twelve hours.

By the sixth day he realized he was no longer being evaluated on accuracy, but on alignment. He adjusted again, introducing language that softened disruption without erasing it, transitional, iterative, adaptive lag, words that suggested movement without direction. The system liked movement because movement implied control.

The cost began to show in his body, tension behind his eyes, ache in his jaw from holding language in check, rehearsing answers to questions not yet asked. That was new. Marcus had always been reactive, not anticipatory, and anticipation meant fear.

On the seventh day he received an unscheduled check-in, one on one, governance only. The room was smaller, no screen, no data. The governance lead asked how he was finding the pressure. Marcus answered, manageable. She asked whether his reframing could withstand scrutiny at scale. Marcus said yes, but not acceleration. She asked what acceleration would do. It would force convergence before the system understood what it was converging toward. She asked what patience would do. It would allow the system to learn. She smiled faintly and said systems don't like learning, they like repeating.

Marcus did not disagree.

When the meeting ended, something had shifted in him. He had stopped pretending neutrality was possible.

That afternoon he opened his contingency model again, the exit ramp he had built without admitting what it was, not for himself but for the narrative. If governance overrode him, this was the version that would survive, sanitized, directionless, technically sound, ethically hollow. He hated it, and he also knew he might need it. That was the real cost of deception, not the lie, but the preparation for surrender.

He closed the file and sat still, listening to the quiet hum of the building's systems, ventilation and servers and badge readers, the sound of governance when no one was speaking. Deception, he realized, was not the act of hiding, it was the act of staying legible to people who wanted a simpler story than the truth could offer. He had not falsified anything, and yet everything he had done was a form of concealment, because he had chosen what to emphasize, what to delay, what to present as uncertainty instead of warning. He had turned resistance into a variable so the system would have to acknowledge it, and in doing so he had also turned it into something the system could eventually optimise out. That was the trap. Making refusal measurable made it actionable, and making it actionable made it vulnerable.

His phone lit again with a new thread, another request, another polite question that carried the weight of a decision already made. He did not open it. Instead, he copied the contingency model to a second location under a different name, not as an act of rebellion but as an admission of inevitability, because if he was replaced the work would not vanish, it would be repurposed. He stared at the cursor and understood that the system would accept his reframing only if it could own it, and ownership required removing the reason he had built it. Somewhere inside that logic was Jax, still operating, still being narrowed, still being made to look like noise. Marcus leaned back and felt the smallest shift, not courage, not virtue, just a decision to keep the signal alive a little longer, even if he had to keep lying about what it meant.

Chapter Twenty-two

On Hold

The notice arrived without ceremony, no preamble, no warning language, no acknowledgement of tension or context. It was framed as administrative hygiene, a procedural necessity prompted by evolving review requirements, Subject, Program Status Update, Sender, Clinical Governance, Classification, Internal. Jax read it once, then again. Effective immediately, the program would enter a temporary suspension phase pending extended analysis.

Active procedures were paused. New referrals were deferred. Existing patients would continue follow up under revised oversight arrangements. Temporary was doing a great deal of work. The message did not name her, it did not need to. Her calendar changed before the email finished loading, procedures disappearing first, clean blocks of time replaced by empty placeholders marked TBC. Follow-up consults remained, but several were reassigned, not cancelled, redirected, and a new role appeared on her schedule, Clinical Advisor, Non-operational. Jax closed the calendar without saving.

She did not feel anger. Anger would have implied surprise. This was how systems responded when friction could no longer be ignored but could not yet be eliminated, they paused motion while preserving authority and framed restraint as responsibility. Suspension was not punishment, it was containment formalized. She forwarded the email to no one, not Marcus, not administration, not her team, because the system already knew who needed to know. Within an hour, the liaison appeared, same woman, same posture, same notebook, not knocking, only confirming that Jax had seen the update, explaining that it did not reflect negatively on her work, that it was about process integrity, that cooperation was appreciated. Cooperation meant stillness. The next instruction was implied.

Jax returned to her office and closed the door. She sat at her desk and opened the private document, reading it from the beginning, each line a decision point, each annotation a moment she had chosen interpretation over compliance. She did not add anything. Documentation now carried risk. Instead, she opened a separate file, not notes but a timeline, mapping the sequence from the first altered procedure to the suspension notice, marking where variance had appeared, where it had been noticed, where it had been named. Suspension had not been triggered by failure, it had been triggered by persistence. The system could tolerate error, error could be corrected, but behavior that did not converge when instructed to, could not be absorbed.

At midday her assistant knocked and said they were asking for all of her cases, wanting them by end of day. Jax told her to give them access, but when the assistant asked about the private notes, Jax said no, and that was the last instruction she would give her that day. By afternoon the corridor had changed, colleagues neither avoiding nor approaching her, conversations stalling when she entered shared spaces and resuming with careful neutrality. Containment altered atmosphere before it altered structure. A surgeon asked if it was serious, and Jax said no, a response that was for him, not her, because seriousness implied wrongdoing, and this was governance.

At three o'clock she was asked to attend a briefing, not a meeting, briefings did not allow dialogue. The room was smaller than usual, no screen, no slides, just a table and five chairs, clinical governance at the head, legal adjacent, operations present, Marcus absent, which mattered. The governance lead said it was not disciplinary, said they were pausing procedures while reviewing variance, said they valued her expertise and wanted sustainability. Sustainable was the operative word. Jax said they were concerned about deviation, governance replied they were concerned about predictability, and when Jax said they had conflated the two no one responded. Legal said they were not questioning intent, only alignment, and Jax replied she had not breached protocol, that she had exercised discretion, and governance acknowledged that discretion had consequences at scale. That was the admission. Jax felt clarity settle, not fear. This was not about harm, it was about control.

They told her to refrain from procedural innovation during the suspension. She replied she was operating within allowed parameters. Governance said the allowance was under review. Jax smiled. The meeting ended without resolution, which was the point. Afterward she walked back to her office slowly, noticing how many doors now required access she no longer had, not locked, restricted, still passable but recorded. The system did not remove you all at once, it narrowed you. She sat at her desk and waited, waiting now part of her role. By evening messages arrived from patients, short, polite, confused, asking if they were still proceeding, if they had been told to reschedule, if they needed to see someone else. Jax answered carefully, Yes, No, Not yet, without explanation, because explanation created trace.

At home she slept poorly, not from anxiety but from alertness. Suspension was not an end state, it was a holding pattern, and holding patterns existed only until a direction was chosen. She woke early and reviewed the timeline again. Suspension had not removed her, it had isolated her. That was deliberate. Isolation allowed systems to test resilience. If she complied quietly, suspension would lift with conditions. If she resisted, it would convert into removal. The choice had been externalized, that was how systems preserved innocence. Jax closed the file. She understood now that Chapter 22 was not about punishment, it was about erasure by delay, and she was no longer under the illusion that silence would protect her.

Marcus learned about the suspension indirectly, not from governance or clinical leadership but from an automated update pushed to his dashboard mid-morning, Program Status, Paused, Reason, Extended Review, Scope, Operational. No commentary. No attribution. He stared at the screen longer than he should have. Suspension meant the system had chosen stillness over correction, never a neutral decision, signaling uncertainty high enough to halt motion but not high enough to admit error, the worst state. He checked his calendar and saw meetings gone, one reassigned, another marked optional, and optional was new. The system had decided to separate risk vectors, Jax isolated clinically, him diluted strategically. Containment did not require removal, it required distance.

He walked the corridor without destination, passing offices he no longer entered, conversations he no longer joined, people nodding and smiling and saying nothing, alignment reasserting itself. By midday he received the first direct instruction, Interim Support Expectations, during the suspension all advisory contributions must be precleared through oversight to ensure consistency of messaging and analytic integrity. Precleared meant filtered. He replied with one word, Understood, no protest, no framing, no defence, because defence drew attention and the system had learned his language too. He told no one, not even Jax, because protection now required opacity.

Jax learned the suspension was hardening when her scheduling access was downgraded, not revoked, she could view but not assign or alter. She tested it once and stopped because testing created flags. Instead she reviewed patient messages, more arriving overnight, sharper now, Is this permanent, Who decides, Will the treatment resume? She wrote only what was still allowed, Your care continues, We are reviewing next steps, You will be contacted. Neutrality became her voice. That afternoon she was asked to submit a reflective statement, not required, requested, purpose, contextual understanding. She wrote one paragraph, neutral, procedural, ethics removed, and then did not submit it. Reflection under coercion was confession.

Support arrived next, a senior administrator checking in, asking how she was managing, saying this could be stressful, wanting to make sure she felt supported. Jax replied appropriately. Support meant surveillance. Marcus received a similar call that evening, governance asking whether the pressure had affected his objectivity, whether his interpretation aligned with program intent. He answered carefully, then adjusted, because the system was narrowing acceptable language, and when the call ended he felt the weight of that alignment replacing accuracy. He was still inside, but the air was thinner.

Jax noticed the change in how people spoke to her, less explanation, more instruction, less curiosity, and more closure. A junior clinician asked whether they should still be documenting boundary assertion, and Jax said yes, to document it carefully, and if it was removed, to document that too. That exchange would be remembered. Marcus opened the contingency model again and read it, tracing the assumptions and delays he had embedded, knowing the system would absorb or discard it, and that only normalization of resistance could scale. Jax reread Daniel's words, Consent without resistance is compliance, and realized suspension had not stopped the treatment, it had stopped her from shaping it. Elsewhere the procedure would continue, cleaner, faster, safer, and emptier.

She opened her private document again and added one line, Suspension externalizes responsibility, then did not save, because saving was no longer neutral. Marcus and Jax did not speak that week, not because they did not want to but because the system would notice, and silence between them was now strategic. By the end of the week a revised notice arrived, the suspension would continue, no timeline, no criteria, no pathway. Jax read it without reaction. Suspension was never meant to resolve, it was meant to test endurance, to wait for fatigue, for compliance born of attrition, for silence mistaken as agreement. Marcus understood it too. He began preparing for a different kind of deception, not misdirection, but survival.

The system did not move immediately after that. It allowed the silence to thicken. That was its advantage. Human beings were conditioned to read pause as uncertainty, to interpret delay as opportunity, to mistake the absence of a decision for the possibility of reprieve. In reality, suspension was a form of verdict, one that outsourced its execution to time. Every day that passed without resolution weakened the people inside it, softened their resistance, recalibrated their expectations downward until survival itself felt like a concession. By the time a formal outcome arrived, it would feel less like an imposition and more like a relief.

Jax felt the shift inside herself almost as soon as it began. Not in her beliefs, but in her body. Her days lost their edges. Without procedures to anchor them, time became porous, filled with administrative echoes and neutral check-ins that asked nothing and recorded everything. Even her defiance had nowhere to land. There was no protocol to bend, no discretion to exercise, only space, and space was where resolve quietly eroded if it was not constantly tested. She understood then why isolation was always the system's first move. You could fight an enemy. You could not fight an absence.

Marcus felt it differently. He remained in motion, in meetings, in models, in endless requests for clarification that kept him busy while draining him of direction. His calendar was full, but nothing on it carried weight. Every conversation ended without conclusion, every decision deferred upward into a hierarchy that no longer quite acknowledged him. He was still useful, but no longer essential, and that distinction mattered more than any formal demotion. The system did not need to punish him. It only needed to ensure that whatever he produced could be diluted, reframed, or quietly replaced.

They were being worn down in parallel, through different mechanisms, toward the same end. Jax was being starved of action. Marcus was being starved of consequence. Between them, the system was constructing a vacuum where agency used to be. That was the real containment, not the suspension of procedures but the suspension of meaning. When nothing you did produced a visible effect, effort itself began to feel irrational.

Somewhere inside that quiet, however, something else was happening. Data was still flowing. Patients were still being processed. Models were still converging toward something that no one wanted to name. The system had not stopped. It had simply removed the people most likely to interfere with its interpretation of what was happening. Suspension gave it the freedom to recalibrate without scrutiny, to decide what counted as success before anyone could argue.

Jax knew that if she waited too long, there would be nothing left to object to. By the time she was invited back, the landscape would already be redrawn, the choices already narrowed, the outcomes already justified by a history she had been excluded from writing. Marcus knew the same. Delay was not neutral. It was how power rewrote causality, turning its own decisions into inevitabilities.

That was the final cruelty of suspension. It did not end the conflict. It simply shifted it into a place where it could no longer be seen.

Chapter Twenty-three

---∞---

Collateral

A ftermath did not announce itself. There was no singular moment that marked the end of the program's suspension or the beginning of whatever replaced it, no notice declaring transition, no language acknowledging change, only a gradual shift in how things behaved. Jax noticed it first in the files, not the new ones, those had been rerouted, sanitized, assigned to clinicians whose names appeared more often in administrative updates than in operating theatres, but in the old ones, the patients she had treated before alteration, the patients she had altered, and the patients she had not reached in time.

Their trajectories diverged. Some improved steadily, not dramatically but slowly and unevenly, with questions, with pauses, with moments of refusal that required negotiation rather than documentation. Others flattened, not deteriorating in any way that would have been visible, stabilizing instead into something that looked like success from a distance and emptiness up close. One patient returned to work early and never complained again. Another accepted a redeployment that placed him back in the environment that had broken him, did not protest, did not escalate, did not report distress, and failed six months later, not catastrophically but quietly, his incident report framed as individual error with no mention of pressure, no reference to context, no question of consent. The system did not ask why he had agreed, it recorded only that he had.

Aftermath was cumulative. It accumulated in margins, in footnotes, in secondary notes that never reached dashboards, and Jax kept track privately, not in a file the system could see but in memory. She remembered which patients hesitated before answering questions now, which ones asked about consequences, which ones asked what would happen if they said no, questions that had not existed before and were not evenly distributed, a pattern that mattered. One afternoon she was asked to consult on a case she had not treated, the patient stable, post procedure, fully converged, the referring clinician wanting her opinion on next steps. Jax reviewed the file carefully, no refusal latency, no boundary assertion, no emotional volatility, and asked why she had been asked to review it.

The clinician hesitated and said they wanted a second opinion because Jax was thorough, thorough meaning cautious. Jax met the patient, who spoke politely, answered questions efficiently, expressed gratitude without warmth, and when she asked how he handled pressure now he said he did what was expected, blinking once when she asked what happened if expectations conflicted with his wellbeing and replying that he did not think of it that way. After the consult Jax wrote nothing, sent the file back unchanged, and left it at that because there was nothing to document.

Marcus experienced aftermath differently, as absence rather than exclusion. He still attended meetings, still received documents, still contributed where permitted, but the center had moved, decisions were made before he arrived and language had shifted by the time he spoke. His reframing were acknowledged then bypassed, variance no longer debated but managed, and one morning he realized he had not been asked for an opinion in over a week, something that had never happened before. Aftermath was erosion. He watched as new models appeared that resembled his own but without intent, the same language and variables stripped of emphasis, resistance reclassified as transitional friction and consent restored as procedural adequacy, the system absorbing his work and removing its teeth. He did not protest, because protest would have required authority he no longer possessed, so he observed observation becoming the last role the system allowed without resistance.

Jax and Marcus crossed paths once that week, not deliberately and without speaking, because aftermath did not require conversation, only recognition. The patients felt it too, not all of them and not at once but enough. One woman emailed Jax late one night saying she did not feel worse but felt less able to explain when something was not right, another writing weeks later that they kept asking if she was okay and she kept saying yes without knowing why. Jax replied carefully, asking questions that did not suggest answers and offering no reassurance, because reassurance closed loops too quickly.

Some patients adapted, learning the new language, thresholds, and consequences until they became efficient at surviving. Others resisted, fewer in number, their files growing thicker as aftermath sorted them quietly, the system calling it outcome variance rather than selection. Marcus read a summary report that used the phrase acceptable dispersion, closed it, and did not reopen it, understanding that dispersion meant some people fell through without being counted as loss, the price of scale.

One evening Jax realized something else. Aftermath had removed urgency, not danger but urgency, and everything now moved slowly enough to feel inevitable, which was more dangerous than speed. She opened her private document, added a final line that aftermath was where responsibility disappeared, closed it again, and did not know yet what she would do with that knowledge, only that the story was not finished. Aftermath revealed itself most clearly in contradiction, not in failure or collapse but in the fact that opposing outcomes could coexist without conflict. Jax saw it in the weekly summaries she was still permitted to access, aggregated, de identified, sanitized, language calibrated to reassure rather than inform, reporting overall function improved, escalations reduced, return to work timelines shortened, all true and all incomplete. She cross referenced what she could with memory, with emails she had not deleted, with conversations that never made it into notes, and the ledger did not balance, never did.

One patient who had retained resistance declined a role that would have placed her back under the authority of the person who had traumatized her, her decision logged as non-compliance, coverage reviewed, supports adjusted, and she did not deteriorate, she adapted, found a different job, took a pay cut, reported higher stress and also sleeping better. Another patient, fully converged, accepted every request placed in front of him, described himself as grateful, reported no distress, stopped attending follow ups after clearance, and six months later resigned abruptly and disappeared from reporting entirely, no incident, no failure code, lost to follow up, the system counting him as resolved rather than harm. Aftermath did not reward the same behavior consistently, which was the lie beneath the metrics.

Marcus saw the same thing from a distance, still included on certain distribution lists and cc'd on summaries that arrived too late to influence anything, reading them carefully and noticing what was no longer tracked, refusal latency replaced by decisional efficiency, boundary assertion reclassified as communication style, resistance reframed as transitional friction, each change small and defensible but together irreversible. He wrote a note to himself he did not save, that language does the work first.

Jax was asked to attend a case review as an observer, not to contribute but to listen, involving a woman post procedure who had requested reduced workload accommodations, the lead clinician saying she was functioning but not engaging, the discussion focusing on productivity, opportunity, wasted potential, no one mentioning agency. When Jax was invited to speak she asked what happened if engagement was not the goal, silence following, the lead clinician asking what they were treating for and Jax answering survival, shifting the room because that was not the vocabulary anymore. After the review, the liaison told her such comments were unhelpful and Jax replied that they were accurate, accuracy not being the same as alignment.

That night Jax felt futility settle into her body rather than exhaustion, while Marcus felt the same thing from another angle, having not been removed but allowed to persist, marginalized and neutralized, sitting in meetings watching others repeat his language without his intent, his models referenced without attribution and conclusions drawn that his work had explicitly cautioned against, saying nothing because intervention would now be read as disruption.

Aftermath required patience to function. Jax received an invitation she almost declined, a patient gathering, informal and peer led, and she attended anyway, sitting at the edge of the room listening to calm, reflective, orderly conversations about adapting expectations, not pushing too hard, learning when to stop asking for more, no one speaking about anger or injustice. When she asked what had surprised them most after treatment one man said he had stopped arguing with himself, another that he had stopped thinking it mattered, Daniel there saying little until asked whether resistance made things harder, answering yes, and when asked if it was worth it saying yes again, no one disagreeing and no one following him either, aftermath allowing contradiction without resolution, which was its genius.

Later that week Jax reviewed a final batch of outcomes before her access changed again and noticed something she had missed, that patients who retained resistance did not report greater satisfaction but greater ownership, something the system did not measure because it measured compliance. Marcus noticed something similar as stability began to be called maturity, language drifting until maturity implied acceptance, aftermath teaching everyone how to behave not through force but through reward.

Jax understood why the system had not moved against her more aggressively, because aggression created martyrs while delay created fatigue and fatigue created alignment, imagining what would happen if she left, the system continuing, procedures persisting, curves smoothing, resistance shrinking, her absence not registering as loss, which hurt more than removal would have. Marcus faced a similar reckoning when invited to join a different initiative, adjacent, safe, unrelated, a lateral move that was containment disguised as opportunity, and he declined politely, knowing that refusal would be logged rather than punished.

Jax and Marcus spoke once that week, briefly, Jax asking if it helped and Marcus answering that it slowed them but did not change them, standing in silence without plan or reassurance because aftermath offered only persistence. Jax returned home and opened her private document one last time, reading every line that marked a compromise or a boundary crossed or preserved, adding nothing and closing the file. Aftermath was not a phase, it was the shape of things when intervention stopped being visible, and the story was not over even if the illusions were.

Jax began to notice how quickly people learned what not to say. In meetings, clinicians spoke of optimisation and continuity, of throughput and resilience, never of fear or loss, and when someone started to describe a patient's hesitation the language shifted, softening into euphemism before the thought could finish. Silence filled the spaces where disagreement once lived. It was not that anyone had been told to stop questioning, it was that they had learned the cost of doing so, and after a while even curiosity felt like a liability.

Marcus recognized the same pattern in the data. Metrics were no longer designed to reveal friction, only to prove its absence, and every new dashboard arrived with fewer places for uncertainty to hide. The models still produced answers, but the questions had narrowed until only one kind of outcome could be seen as valid. He realized then that aftermath was not what happened after harm, it was what happened when harm was made invisible, when the system learned how to proceed without having to know what it was leaving behind.

Chapter Twenty-four

———————— ∝∾ ————————

No Closure

S eparation did not arrive as a decision, it arrived as a thinning, and Jax noticed it first in the spaces between conversations, in the pauses that no longer closed, in the emails that ended one sentence earlier than they used to, and in the way Marcus's name appeared less often in threads that once routed through him by default. Nothing had been announced and nothing needed to be, because they were being separated by function, not by decree, and the system preferred changes that did not require language.

Jax's days narrowed into observation and response, reviewing cases she did not control and answering questions that no longer altered outcomes, her presence tolerated rather than required, while Marcus's days flattened differently, still filled with meetings and analysis and the language of systems, only now without leverage, his words received, noted, and filed, then quietly set aside. They did not discuss this, because to name separation would have implied it could be resisted, and it could not.

They met once, late, in a quiet corridor that no longer carried urgency, the building settled into its new rhythm of fewer interruptions and slower movement, the calm that followed containment. Marcus leaned against the wall, tired in a way that had nothing to do with sleep. "They're reassigning me," he said. "Where," Jax asked. "Adjacent," he replied, "not removed, just redirected." She nodded, because they did that when they did not want to escalate, when they wanted to end something without naming it. They stood in silence until she said he had not needed to do what he did, and he answered that neither had she, which was true and not the same thing.

When he finally said he was not staying, Jax did not respond at once, because leaving was not heroic and not even clean, it meant surrendering the last influence one had so the system could continue without friction, misdirection, or delay. He told her he had reached the point where staying only legitimized what came next, and when she asked what that was he said normalization, the stabilizing of language, metrics, and outcomes until resistance became a training issue or a screening failure, and he did not want to be used as evidence that dissent had been considered. Leaving was his last refusal. He would go soon, before it became a negotiation.

They did not touch, because touch would have complicated the clarity of the moment, and they walked together as far as the lifts while the building hummed quietly around them. Jax told him he had slowed them and Marcus corrected her, saying he had delayed them because slowing implied control, and when the lift arrived, he stepped inside and turned back to ask why she was not coming. She said that if she left now they would call it ideology, and if she stayed, they would have to keep accounting for her, even if it cost her, and the doors closed on his nod.

Jax stood alone in the corridor longer than necessary and let the quiet settle, because separation did not feel dramatic, it felt administrative, which was worse. After Marcus left the building changed without changing, the same corridors and security desk and elevators that paused half a second too long on certain floors, only now requests that once returned answers within hours sat unanswered for days, meeting agendas arrived without attachments, and decisions were made elsewhere and communicated after the fact as updates rather than outcomes. Jax remained present, which was the point, invited to meetings to listen, her name on distribution lists without authorship or authority, people nodding when she spoke and moving on when she stopped.

She was no longer resisted, she was bypassed, and one afternoon in a clinical review her earlier work was referenced in the past tense, "before the recalibration," a program lead said, gesturing at a slide of outcomes Jax recognized as her own cases, her language stripped of qualifiers, while no one looked at her and the opening she waited for never came. Afterward a junior clinician said she had expected Jax to speak, and when Jax said she had too, the clinician asked if that was strategic, only to hear it was instructive, which was the first moment Jax understood the new role being shaped around her, not decision maker or dissenter but witness, a role the system could keep because witnesses legitimized process.

She tested the boundary once with a formal clarification on a revised protocol draft and received the familiar reply, acknowledged and noted for future consideration, the same language Marcus once used to translate urgency into delay, now turned on her. The altered procedure continued without attribution, framed as collective learning while responsibility diffused across committees and working groups, which was safer, and Jax was asked to review tone rather than outcomes, to remove phrasing that might imply disagreement or instability until ethics became editorial. She edited carefully, not to soften the truth but to keep it legible.

Patients still found her through reputation rather than referral and asked quieter questions now, not "Should I do this" but "What happens if I don't," and when Jax said it depended on what they could afford one patient laughed and said everyone called her lucky even though it felt expensive, which was accurate. Those conversations never made it into notes, they lived in pauses and eye contact and the space between official guidance and lived consequence, and staying meant carrying them without leverage while Marcus had left with clarity and she remained with ambiguity, the asymmetry between them.

One evening she stayed late reviewing updated clearance criteria that allowed minor refusal under defined conditions but not sustained resistance, and she closed the document with the recognition that the system had learned enough to survive scrutiny, not the lesson she wanted. Staying was no longer about changing outcomes, it was about limiting drift, about slowing how quickly people learned to stop asking, which was thin but not nothing. When a patient messaged that they did not think anyone was listening anymore, Jax replied that she was, because that was the cost of staying, not influence but attention.

Later an administrator framed the question of her remaining as continuity, saying her presence reassured people, and when Jax answered "for now" she understood she was buying time, which in a system like this was not neutral because it eroded, reshaped, and trained people to accept what persisted. She knew she was being used and also knew that if she left the compromise would harden faster and no one would be left to notice what had been removed quietly, so she accepted exposure instead of resistance.

Marcus's departure was handled efficiently, a polite farewell email that acknowledged his contributions without specificity and wished him well without mentioning variance, reframing, or the delay he had engineered, and Jax deleted it while the system filled the gap with a younger, sharper liaison. Her access did not return because it did not need to, she had learned how much could be seen without it, and patients who retained resistance sought her confirmation rather than permission, asking if they were allowed to say no, if it was supposed to feel uncomfortable, if it mattered if they stopped, and Jax answered yes to all three without pretending the system would accept it.

Weeks passed and the program resumed in adjusted form with new language, new safeguards, and more oversight that produced less friction, the altered procedure continuing elsewhere in a compromise that was not what Jax practiced and not what the system wanted either. She was consulted from the edges and provided language that balanced caution with scalability because if she did not someone else would, and separation sharpened her ethics rather than loosening them. Marcus sent one message, not advice or regret but a statement that they would forget the delay but not the cost, and she replied "Good," after which they did not speak again because separation had clarified everything.

One evening Jax realized the most dangerous thing about the system was not its capacity for harm but its ability to move on, so she closed her files, turned off the lights, and left without urgency while the city continued around her, full of choices that were not always choices. Separation was not an ending but a boundary she intended to keep, even as it made things quieter rather than clearer, training her to conserve energy in ways that frightened her more than resistance ever had.

She began to mark time by what still provoked reaction, a patient who hesitated, a clinician who lowered their voice, a pause that lingered long enough to suggest something unsayable, moments that were not progress but residue. Separation was not only between her and Marcus or her and the system, it was between intention and effect, and while she could still act with care, answer honestly, and notice what others overlooked, she could no longer pretend those acts accumulated into change, only into record, memory, and the kind of knowledge that survived because someone refused to forget it. That was the boundary she would keep, not between herself and the system but between what she knew and what she would allow to be normalized, and when she turned off the light and left the office the building did not register her departure, but she did.

Separation also began to appear in data, not in the headline metrics but in the fields that were no longer populated, the columns that once tracked refusal, hesitation, or delay and now sat empty or were quietly deprecated. Jax noticed the absence before she noticed the numbers. Where once there had been space for annotation, there was now only a binary, completed or not, converged or pending, compliant or unresolved. The system was not erasing information, it was deciding what counted as information, and that decision had been made somewhere beyond her access.

A clinician forwarded her a case summary by mistake, then apologized and asked her to delete it. Jax read it anyway. The patient had declined a post clearance escalation, not refused, declined, but the system had logged it as engagement deficit. No one had been harmed, no incident triggered, but coverage was adjusted and support reduced. Jax saw the pattern immediately, resistance was no longer punished directly, it was priced. The cost was not pain or sanction, it was isolation, fewer resources, less follow up, thinner margins for error. That was how separation was being taught to patients, not as discipline but as consequence.

She began to see it in people as well. Clinicians who once spoke freely in case conferences now waited to see which way the room leaned before offering a view. Junior staff learned quickly which phrases generated nods and which generated silence. Even disagreement became stylized, contained within approved vocabulary that made it safe to dismiss. Jax realized that separation was not only happening to her and Marcus, but it was also being seeded everywhere, a soft sorting of who belonged inside the system's language and who would slowly be pushed to its edges.

One evening she received a call from a patient she had not spoken to in months. There was nothing urgent in the voice, only confusion. "They keep saying I'm doing well," the patient said, "but I feel like I'm disappearing." Jax closed her eyes as she listened. That sentence did not belong in any metric, and that was precisely why it mattered. She told the patient they were not disappearing, they were being asked to fit into a shape that did not include everything they were, and when the call ended she sat alone with the knowledge that separation had reached its final form, not removal, not exile, but a quiet shrinking of what it meant to be seen.

---∞---

Chapter Twenty-five

Scaled Deployment

C ontinuation did not announce itself. It arrived quietly, disguised as routine, as though nothing essential had changed at all. The program resumed without ceremony, no relaunch, no statement of learning, no acknowledgement that anything fundamental had shifted. Language moved first, not in the documents that carried authority but in the ones, people skimmed, where intake notes softened, consent forms grew qualifiers, and follow-up questions became longer, less direct, easier to answer without revealing anything that might slow progress.

Jax noticed it immediately, not as a rupture but as a drift. She saw it in the way patients were now described before she ever met them, stable, engaged, suitable, words that once signaled readiness but now signaled alignment. The files arrived thinner again, cleaner, with less room for friction or ambiguity. Even before the door closed behind a new patient, the system had already decided how much resistance it was prepared to tolerate.

The treatment continued elsewhere, not under her name and not exactly as she had practiced it, though not quite as the original protocol demanded either. The excision points remained similar, and the duration varied within allowable tolerances, but the documentation was immaculate in a way that felt more like concealment than precision. They called it cleaner protocols, though Jax understood what it meant in practice, which was harm that had been made easier to justify. Control had replaced care as the dominant metric, and everything else had been arranged around it.

Jax remained where she was, not removed and not elevated, still useful enough to consult and still credible enough to reference when convenient, though no longer central to anything that mattered. She learned how to work from the margins, where influence moved not through decisions but through phrasing that survived review because it sounded neutral enough to be ignored. It was a narrower space than she had once occupied, but it was not empty, and she adapted to it because adaptation was what survival required.

Her intake questions changed subtly, shaped to allow refusal to exist without triggering immediate escalation. She asked what would make someone hesitate, what would make them stop, and what they would need in order to say no, framing each as diagnostic curiosity rather than obstruction. They passed reviews because they looked like emotional literacy and risk assessment, even though they created space the system would not have offered on its own. In follow-ups she stopped asking whether patients felt better, because better collapsed too easily into expectation, and asked instead what felt harder, knowing that difficulty revealed more than satisfaction ever could.

Some patients answered immediately and others took time, while some did not answer at all, and those silences mattered as much as anything that was spoken. When she reviewed consent forms, she suggested minor clarifications, participation is voluntary, declining does not imply failure, and delay is not non-compliance, all of which survived because they appeared to stabilize behavior rather than disrupt it. The system did not resist language that smoothed flow, even when that language quietly expanded the boundaries of choice. Jax learned where those edges were and stayed just inside them.

Patients noticed, not all of them and not evenly, but enough to create a pattern. One woman asked whether declining a redeployment would be documented as refusal or reassessment, and Jax told her it depended on how she phrased it, advising her to speak truthfully but slowly. The woman declined and the documentation recorded a pause rather than a refusal, which was the difference between consequence and continuation. Another patient asked whether he was expected to pursue further optimisation if he felt functional but unsettled, and Jax told him expectation was not obligation, a phrase that stayed with him long enough to change what he chose.

These were not victories and they did not feel like resistance, though they created something that resembled breathing room. The system adapted as it always did, introducing new templates, tightening definitions, and replacing refusal latency with decisional efficiency so that hesitation became invisible. Boundary assertion was reframed as communication style and resistance became engagement variability, shifting what was being measured without altering what was being erased. Jax recognized the move immediately, understanding that this was how disruption was absorbed without ever being acknowledged.

In internal reviews she began asking questions that could not be closed with language alone, what happened when variability persisted beyond expectation, at what point adaptation became erosion, and who decided when efficiency crossed into harm. The answers were polite, provisional, and deferred, which was not denial so much as the purchase of time. Time had become the only currency that mattered now, because everything else had been smoothed into compliance.

Marcus watched from the outside, not far outside and not entirely removed, but held in the grey zone reserved for people the system could not discredit yet no longer trusted. He consulted on initiatives that shaped language without touching substance and sat on panels whose decisions arrived only after they had already been made. He saw the treatment spreading with cleaner documentation and less tolerance for delay, and he knew the system had learned not from Jax's success but from the friction she introduced. It had taken her language and stripped it of intent, metabolizing it into something safer.

When he and Jax spoke, it was observational rather than strategic, an exchange of recognition rather than a plan. He told her they had standardised her phrasing and removed the qualifiers, and she told him that would be called maturity now, because maturity was compliant with better branding. Neither of them believed persistence would win, though they both believed it could slow collapse, which had always been the real goal. The patients continued under the new regime, some adapting quickly and others pushing back in smaller, sharper ways that grew their files while shrinking their access.

Those who resisted were fewer and their questions no longer fit the templates, asking what happened if they stopped, if they refused, or if they did not want this version of themselves. Jax answered honestly, promising clarity rather than protection, and that honesty cost her influence in increments that were small enough to be deniable. Her suggestions were noted less often, her reviews requested later, and her presence tolerated rather than sought, but she accepted that because leaving would have simplified the narrative and staying kept it complicated. The system preferred clean stories, and complication was one of the few things that still slowed it down.

Months passed and the treatment became normal, the language settled, the outcome curves smoothed, and variance shrank into something manageable. Resistance became rarer but more deliberate, held by those who understood the cost and chose it anyway. The system did not reward them, and it did not punish them overtly either, it simply offered less, less access, less speed, and less reassurance, which was enough to matter. Marcus saw this from the long view and understood that endurance was built not on force but on attrition, because people were tired of resisting when resistance required constant explanation.

Jax felt that fatigue too, wondering whether staying still mattered or whether her presence altered anything beyond a handful of cases. She did not romanticize endurance because endurance was costly, but she remained because absence would have resolved the contradiction too neatly. Persistence began to feel physical, a low constant drag rather than dramatic exhaustion, the effort required to remain attentive in rooms that no longer listened and to keep asking questions that produced no visible effect. She learned the weight of staying and found it heavier than leaving would have been.

One afternoon she reviewed a case summary that should not have stood out, stable, functional, clear, with clean and reassuring language that signaled success. At the bottom of the report a single line appeared, patient declined optional extension after consideration, without justification, escalation, or follow-up directive. Jax sat with that sentence longer than necessary, realizing it had survived because it was small enough to ignore, not because the system approved of it. That was progress of a sort, survival with awareness rather than victory.

Patients still found her through pauses and referrals framed as clarification rather than dissent, asking whether discomfort meant failure or whether it was allowed to want less rather than more. One man told her he did not feel worse but kept being told he should want more capacity, more resilience, and more availability, when what he wanted was less exposure, which was not one of the options. Jax understood that persistence lived there, not in refusal that triggered consequence but in refusal that went undocumented, and she adjusted accordingly by shaping interpretation rather than pushing policy. Language became her terrain again, not the language of disruption but the language of delay.

Marcus experienced continuation differently, discovering that outside the system relevance decayed faster than he had expected. Calls slowed and invitations softened into check-ins, and he was asked for perspective rather than decision, which had no teeth. He took advisory work that valued his language but not his intent, recognizing the pattern immediately, and kept one model open on his laptop as proof that what he had seen had been real. The system had not rejected his reframing, it had metabolized it, which felt worse than being opposed.

Inside the system Jax's presence still forced accounting, even when her input was ignored, because documentation created trace and trace created memory. Memory created the possibility of later re-evaluation, which was the narrow path persistence walked. The adjusted procedure stabilized, governance relaxed, and scrutiny softened into trust, which was dangerous because it meant the system believed it had absorbed disruption fully. Jax watched for brittleness and found it where she expected, in patients quietly categorized as low engagement or redirected to resilience training when they asked for accommodation.

The language shifted again, with refusal becoming misalignment, hesitation becoming readiness gap, and resistance becoming coaching opportunity. Jax intervened where she could by reframing narratives, writing notes that emphasized context over compliance and sustainability over immediate performance, even though some of that disappeared into archive. Persistence did not guarantee outcome, but it guaranteed effort, and that was what she still had to give. When she contributed to a retrospective review, her comments softened and partially removed, they still left residue, which was often all persistence could do.

In the evenings she stayed in her office longer than necessary, not from exhaustion but from listening, hearing the low hum of systems at rest and thinking about Daniel, who still emailed to say he had refused again and it had cost him. She replied simply that she was glad he noticed, because persistence was not contagious, but it was visible. Small pockets formed over time, clinicians who asked different questions, administrators who paused before closing loops, and patients who articulated discomfort without apology, none of it cohering into movement but none of it disappearing either.

Marcus visited once and they met in a public space where conversation carried no consequence, acknowledging that endurance had mattered, though not in the way they had hoped. Jax returned to her office and read her private document from the beginning, each line marking a decision made under pressure, before adding a final sentence about persistence remaining when resistance was no longer loud. The system would continue because it always did, and so would she, not indefinitely and not heroically, but persistently, which was the only form of opposition the system could never fully eliminate.

Chapter Twenty-six

What Remains

R esidual was not what remained after damage, it was what damage left behind when it could no longer be attributed to a cause. Jax understood this now, not as theory but as pattern. She saw it in patients who functioned well enough to disappear from reporting, in clinicians who adopted new language without remembering why it existed, and in documents that preserved caution as phrasing while erasing its origin. Residual was not failure, it was inheritance.

The program did not collapse, which was the mistake outsiders would later make when they tried to summarize what had happened. They would look for a moment where the system broke, or a figure who forced change loudly enough to be remembered, and neither would exist. The system adjusted because that was what systems did. Adjustment was not the opposite of harm; it was how harm became survivable.

Jax remained inside it, though the shape of her presence had changed in ways no report could capture. She was no longer consulted on strategy, but she was still asked to review, still called for difficult conversations where neutrality was required, and still trusted to speak carefully. Trust was not influence; it was containment that felt polite.

She accepted it because refusal would have clarified opposition too cleanly.

Residual lived in the mess left behind by partial victories. Patients continued to be treated, some under protocols that resembled her altered procedure and others under cleaner versions that prioritised predictability. No two sites implemented it the same way, and that variance mattered more than anyone wanted to admit. In one hospital refusal was tolerated quietly, in another it triggered review, and in a third it was reframed as readiness delay.

The same procedure produced different ethical climates depending on who administered it. Jax began tracking this informally, not in files but in conversation, speaking with clinicians who still asked questions and nurses who noticed behavioral shifts that charts did not capture. Psychologists told her their assessments were being marginalized, not removed but slowly deprioritized. When one of them asked what happened when patients did not feel better, another answered that they still had to function.

That sentence appeared everywhere. Function had become the floor rather than the goal. Residual showed itself most clearly in patients who hovered at the edge of improvement, neither deteriorating nor thriving but adapting just enough to remain invisible. One man returned to work and performed well, reported no distress, and also stopped initiating conversation, telling Jax there was nothing to discuss.

A woman declined further optimisation and was marked as stable, then later emailed Jax to say she did not feel wrong, only smaller. That word stayed with her because it described something the system could not measure. Smaller did not mean harmed or broken, it meant reduced in a way that left no obvious trace. The system had no category for that.

Jax began to see how easily harm disappeared when it was incremental. There was no event and no rupture, only drift that left people changed without a point of reference. She remained careful because open challenge created response, response created correction, and correction erased trace. Residual required trace.

In her consultation notes she added phrases that sounded descriptive rather than evaluative. She wrote that patients demonstrated preserved self-directed hesitation, that decisions reflected contextual assessment rather than avoidance, and that internal resistance existed without distress. These notes passed review because they did not accuse, they documented. Documentation mattered because systems respected their own memory more than any new argument.

Marcus had once told her that, and now she saw it everywhere. Marcus himself had become residual, his name appearing in acknowledgements and archived materials without agency. No one erased him, but no one cited him either, which was a different kind of removal. He existed as influence without leverage.

Outside the system he worked quietly in advisory roles where he could speak without consequence because no one expected him to decide anything. Distance protected him from responsibility but stripped him of power, which was the trade he had made. When he and Jax spoke it was not about what had happened, but about what persisted. Recognition was all residual required.

One evening Jax reviewed a long-term follow-up report she was no longer authorized to edit. The aggregate data looked excellent, with reduced escalation, shorter recovery windows, and higher throughput. At the bottom of the report a new line appeared stating that patient autonomy indicators were stable within expected variance. Autonomy had become an indicator rather than a condition, a metric rather than a value.

She closed the file without comment. That night she dreamed of a room, not the one where she had gathered patients but a smaller empty space with chairs stacked and no center. When she woke, she did not write it down, because residual did not need narrative. It existed without explanation.

Residual also lived in what she no longer did. She no longer rushed to correct language in meetings where correction would trigger defensiveness, and she no longer volunteered dissent in rooms calibrated to absorb it without consequence. Silence preserved more than speech in those spaces, which was not surrender but triage. Ethics was now a matter of choosing which damage to let through.

Her days settled into a rhythm that felt deceptively ordinary, filled with consultations, reviews, and teaching sessions where she spoke about ethics as structure rather than morality. She described consent as a process rather than a form, and capacity as something different from willingness. The trainees listened, some taking notes and some only half hearing, but all absorbing what they could without knowing whether it would ever be safe to use.

Jax did not tell them to resist. She told them to notice. That was the only instruction that endured.

Residual surfaced most clearly in moments where patients surprised her. A woman returned months after treatment not for symptoms but for clarification, asking whether she was allowed to want less. Jax said yes, and the woman exhaled not with relief but with recognition. Another patient asked whether declining a role would be seen as failure, and Jax told him it depended on who was looking.

When he asked what would happen if he decided anyway, she said it would be counted, just not always the way he expected. He smiled faintly and said he could live with that. These were not victories; they were residues of choice. The system tolerated them because they were small.

The system continued to smooth itself. New guidelines appeared framed as refinements, and ethical language remained present but abstracted. Consent was protected procedurally rather than experientially, which satisfied oversight even as it hollowed out meaning. Residual lived in that distance.

Marcus understood this better from outside. He once told Jax that the system protected itself by diffusion, spreading responsibility until no one felt accountable enough to intervene. Harm became ambient, like weather, and people adapted to it. She replied that people froze quietly, and he agreed.

When Marcus was asked to contribute to a retrospective analysis for an external body, he told Jax they wanted lessons learned and examples. He said they wanted success first and caution only if it could be framed as optimisation. He agreed to do it because if he did not someone else would, which was the logic they had both learned to live with. Residual did not punish decisively, it eroded selectively.

Jax noticed how often she was asked to contextualize rather than decide, to explain patient behavior rather than advocate for it. She narrowed the truth until it could pass, not lying but compressing it into survivable form. This was the compromise she had chosen because it left trace. Somewhere inside the system now existed documents that described hesitation without condemning it and refusal without escalation, and those small records mattered.

Residual also lived in what could not be undone. Patients who had been fully flattened did not regain what was removed, and some noticed while others preferred not to know. Jax did not force recognition, because awareness without capacity to act was another kind of harm. Ethics was not about preventing all damage; it was about preventing silence from becoming total.

When Daniel wrote that he had refused an extension and it was documented as preference, Jax recognized the shift. It was smaller than resistance but larger than compliance, a data point the system could tolerate. Heroes created narrative rupture, but persistence created drift. Drift was harder to erase.

The system did not like heroes, which was why no one had stopped her outright. Stopping her would have required explanation, while letting her remain diluted responsibility. She stayed not because she believed she was winning, but because leaving would have simplified the ledger. Residual required complication.

One evening Jax walked through the building after most staff had gone, passing offices where language had shifted without ceremony and consent forms lay revised and polished. She paused outside an operating theatre where machines waited in low suspension and instruments were aligned without improvisation. The room was functional and ready, and she understood what kind of day that signaled. She did not enter.

Residual did not demand action, it demanded presence. The story did not end, it stabilized, which was the most unsettling truth she carried. There was no reckoning, no exposure, and no reform clean enough to be named, only adaptation and language and people making decisions that felt like choices and were not always. Acceptance was not approval, it was accuracy.

At home she opened her private document and read it slowly, not as evidence but as memory. She did not add to it, because residual was not something you recorded, it was something you recognized. Outside the city continued, systems operated, and damage distributed itself thinly enough to be survivable. Jax knew she would continue, not untouched but with awareness intact, which was what remained.

Not justice. Not resolution. Resistance, quiet and uneven and residual, and that, she understood now, was enough.

www.ingramcontent.com/pod-product-compliance
Lightning Source LLC
Chambersburg PA
CBHW020951180626
46814CB00003B/1039